G000122890

Tangled Webs

Tangled Webs

Bryan Roskams

Copyright © 2011 by Bryan Roskams.

Library of Congress Control Number:		2011917877
ISBN:	Hardcover	978-1-4653-7306-9
	Softcover	978-1-4653-7305-2
	Ebook	978-1-4653-7307-6

All rights reserved. No part of this book may be reproduced or transmitted in any form or by any means, electronic or mechanical, including photocopying, recording, or by any information storage and retrieval system, without permission in writing from the copyright owner.

This is a work of fiction. Names, characters, places and incidents either are the product of the author's imagination or are used fictitiously, and any resemblance to any actual persons, living or dead, events, or locales is entirely coincidental.

This book was printed in the United States of America.

To order additional copies of this book, contact:
Xlibris Corporation
0-800-644-6988
www.xlibrispublishing.co.uk
Orders@xlibrispublishing.co.uk
302706

CONTENTS

To my sister Brenda for being my original critic.

To my wife Jan for her unfailing support.

CHAPTER 1

THE DECEIT

A blinding flash of lightning zigzagged across the dark horizon directly ahead, ending its tortuous journey in little rivulets of brilliant light. Three seconds later, what started as a slow rumble erupted into a full-scale explosion that spread out in all directions across the sky, signalling another fall of torrential rain. The road was already showing signs of flooding, due to previous cloudbursts, making driving very hazardous, especially so if you were driving in unfamiliar territory. Peter Doddington leant forward over the wheel and squinted through the windscreen in order to catch the sudden twists and turns of the road ahead. Although the headlights were on main beam, cutting a swathe through the blackness of the night, Peter still found it difficult to define where the road ended and the ditches on either side began. Keeping his hand on the steering wheel, his left thumb deftly flicked the wiper's motor too fast, in an effort to divert the waterfall now cascading down the windscreen. To make matters worse, he did not have a clue where he was, relying solely on his sat nav. He had religiously followed its instructions to the letter, despite having misgivings earlier about its accuracy. He glanced at the dashboard clock; it was now nearly 9.30 p.m. He suddenly realised how very tired he felt. Driving for six hours without a break had taken its toll. Apart from being hungry and thirsty, he was desperate for the toilet. Rubbing his eyes to try to keep himself awake, he began to feel very weary and depressed as his mind started to dwell on how much his life had changed since this time last year. He thought he'd had it all, a very good position with British Gas as one of their top design engineers, designing and overseeing the installation and commissioning of pressure reduction stations, not only in the UK but also in different parts of the world, where various governments were always keen to call on the expert knowledge and experience of large British companies. (This business had escalated since the introduction of natural gas into the national grid system in the 1950s.) He had also enjoyed an excellent marriage, shared with an exceptional partner in Shirley, whom he had always trusted implicitly, and two wonderful kids, Jamie, ten, and little Josie, just three. They had all lived in the same detached three-bedroomed house they had bought ten years ago, situated in the little village of Paglesham, nestled adjacent to the river Crouch in the County of Essex. That is, until he came home early one afternoon, completely unexpected, and found Shirley and his best friend Tony Harman, in bed together.

It put him in such a state of utter shock that he turned round and left the room without Shirley or her lover becoming aware of his presence.

It was the catalyst that made him take a good close look at his life, and what he was going to do with his future.

He had, like most people, heard news of infidelities amongst his friends, and indeed in some cases in his extended family, but he had built up an absolute trust in his own partnership with Shirley, so much so, that whenever he was sent to a foreign country to carry out important installations on behalf of his firm, he had always asked Tony to keep an eye on his loved ones, knowing he would be able to concentrate on the exacting and often dangerous briefs that he might encounter during the process of his contract.

The effects of the deceit they had inflicted upon him made him start to question other aspects of his life. If he did not really know his own wife, or his best friend, was there anyone else whom he thought he knew and could trust?

About a month after it happened, he began to lose confidence in his own abilities. He had always been a very competent professional. His peers would come to him for advice, knowing it would be sound. After the discovery, he had doubts about everything.

After the inevitable confrontation, accusations, tears, and apologies, which came thick and fast from all concerned, he came to the painful conclusion that to forgive and forget was something he would never be able to live with, especially as both Shirley and his so-called 'best friend' had, after a lot of pushing, admitted that the affair had been going on for the last three years. The final blow came when he found out that he was not little Josie's biological father.

Up to this period in his life, Peter had had a very *likable* personality, always the first to step up to the front in times of need, to offer help to any of his friends or family. It was his quirky sense of humour that first drew Shirley to him all those years ago. Apart from his tanned good looks and his easy-going manner, he was loyal, honest, and reliable; he spoke his mind, whether it pleased or offended, and definitely did not suffer fools *gladly*. With Peter Doddington, it was classic: what you saw is what you got.

His recent work project had gone very well, both for him and British Gas; it had taken up the last six months of his life to complete and commission a large pressure reduction station, which was now supplying natural gas into the national grid system. He had been lucky to find lovely digs with a family in a small village about twenty miles from Edinburgh, where he had, more or less, become part of the family. Moreover, it was just what he needed at the time, so he threw himself into his work in order to try to stop the pain of losing his family.

Because he wanted to keep as busy as possible, he had requested his next assignment start straightaway. Peter bade his farewells to his hosts and began the long journey to the fishing town of Looe in Cornwall, where he would meet up with the contractors who would then become part of his responsibility for the building of the next pressure reduction station.

It was quite late in the afternoon when he started on his way. He was already tired, and so he did not relish the long journey ahead. He had now been on the road for the best part of six hours and knew he was not going to complete the journey tonight.

CHAPTER 2

THE TWILIGHT ZONE

After travelling another two or three miles, he was forced to slow down to a crawl in order to negotiate a double hairpin bend. Peter suddenly took offence to the DJ going on about some insignificant happening, and he promptly stretched out to turn the radio off at the very moment a lorry came around the next bend towards him. He yanked the wheel hard over to the left in order to avoid a collision and very nearly ended up in the ditch. He heard the scraping of the bushes against the side of the car as he fought to gain control. After swerving to the other side of the road, he managed to get the vehicle going straight. His heart was going nineteen to the dozen, and he felt himself shaking; he shouted out loud every swear word he could think of, which made him feel a lot better. Now with the radio switched off, all he could hear was the constant drumming of the rain on the roof.

The road suddenly widened to reveal a small, old shack of a garage with a single petrol pump outside.

The rain had abated somewhat, and the wiper blades were now coping very well at normal speed.

He swung the car into the tiny space between the road and the pump, the beams of the headlights glistening on the wet surface.

A bell jingled somewhere inside the rusty corrugated walls of the building as the wheels ran over a cable that lay on the forecourt. Peter smiled to himself as the sound triggered a distant memory of long ago, something to do with Shirley, on another journey.

He turned off the headlights, opened the petrol cap, and switched off the engine. On stepping into the cold wet night, he was greeted by a small old man wearing greasy overalls and an old yellow baseball cap pulled down over his forehead. As he drew nearer towards Peter, he held out his hand in a friendly gesture.

'Good evening, sir.' His voice came out as a deep throaty rattle, at the same time trying to catch his breath, consistent with the symptoms which one would expect to find in a chronic asthmatic. Peter was looking at someone in his late seventies.

Bent at the waist at such an angle, it was impossible for him to look where he was going without lifting his head.

Peter took the old man's hand in a firm grip.

'Hello there,' he replied.

'I'd like to fill her up if I may?'

'Sure thing, matey, you're lucky you found me here, I was just about to lock up for the night.' He grinned, retrieving a big bunch of keys from the top pocket of his overalls. He selected one of them, and with a shaky hand inserted it into the padlock. Peter noticed that when the old man turned the key, his knuckles were knurled and prominent to such an extent that he had a job to hold the key and then struggle to insert the nozzle into the tank.

He raised his head to look at Peter.

'We don't get many strangers around these parts. It's a bit off the beaten track.' He paused to draw much-needed air.

'You've come to visit someone, or just passing through?'

Peter let out an embarrassed giggle as he answered, 'To tell you the truth, I am completely and utterly lost.' At which point he had to raise his voice, as the old electric pump drowned any other noise as, with seemingly great effort, it began to suck the fuel from the underground reservoir. He went on to explain briefly that he was on his way to Looe in Cornwall, and that the sat nav had led him astray. The noisy pump went suddenly quiet as the old man finished his chore. He hung the nozzle back on its hook with a slightly puzzled look on his face; he then lifted his head and said, 'Well, I don't know much about those new sorts of fangled things, but I can tell you, you are a long way from Cornwall.' He peered at Peter over the top of his specs with a glint in his eye and leant up against the pump housing.

'You look as though you could do with a good night's sleep. Not only that, it's dark now, and if you need to make it to Cornwall, you've got at least another three hours' driving to do. You are now about five miles from Birmingham.'

Peter lifted his right hand and brought his thumb and middle finger together wearily across his eyes, at the same time drawing in a deep breath and then letting the air expel from his lungs very slowly.

'Yes, mate, I think you're right,' he replied, as he took his wallet from the back pocket of his jeans.

'Do you happen to know of a decent place for the night by any chance?'

The old boy stretched out his hand and took the money Peter offered him, fitted the petrol cap back in its place, and snapped the flap shut. With the money still clasped in his fingers, he lifted his arm, waved up the road, and said, 'Well, as a matter of fact, I do know of a little old pub just about three miles down the road from here. It lay back somewhat away from the road, but you can't miss it, it's called the Devil's Inn.'

Peter didn't notice the strange grin on his face as he said firmly, 'They'll look after you there, my boy!'

Peter thanked the old man and quickly got back on to the road. It had stopped raining, for now at least, and it wouldn't be long before he was sitting down with a pint in his hand and having a bite to eat. The thought suddenly lifted his spirits. He was looking forward to finding the Devil's Inn.

About five miles further on, Peter saw a flickering of lights filtering through the trees a little way ahead and to his right.

Sure enough, he soon found himself alongside a stout oak pole rising twenty feet into the sky, and swinging from an iron bracket was old Satan himself, complete with a three-pronged fork and curved horns, looking down at him with a knowing wicked grin.

The Devil's Inn, as the old man had indicated, lay back from the road by a good hundred yards, and as Peter turned the car into the entrance to the car park, he quickly estimated that the old pub must have been there for two or three hundred years.

As he selected a spot to park, he noticed there were no other vehicles around. Moreover, he gave it no more than just a passing thought that it was a bit unusual for this time in the evening for there to be so few cars around, especially as a pub like this must have to rely on passing trade for its continued success. Peter didn't immediately get out of the car, but he sat there looking at the old building. The headlights lit up the entire front of the place. He noticed that the roof looked as though it had sagged in the middle, and one of the chimney pots was missing from the stack.

The gutters were only about six feet from the ground and were sprouting shoots of grass in selected places along its length; rainwater was running over the top, on to the once beautiful oak window frames, confirming the reason for the extensive rot that was apparent on the sills. A dim light struggled to escape from the other side of the dirty windows. In places, the walls had given up on holding on to the rendering, letting it muster in little mounds on the ground below.

Thinking it a bit strange that the landlord of this quaint old inn could allow it to deteriorate into such a condition, he switched off the lights, stepped out of the car, and made his way to the entrance. The heavy solid oak door made a distinct creaking sound as it swung inwards before he had hardly touched it.

A top-quality red thick pile carpet covered the floor as he stepped inside a spacious low ceiling bar. Through the dim light, he could just make out there were tables and chairs arranged for groups of two to four people.

A piano was being played quietly in one corner, someone was laughing, and it sounded hollow, as though they did not really mean it.

Wondering why he had not noticed them before, he saw quite a lot of people sitting at the tables talking in low tones, while others sat alone staring into space, with half-empty glasses on the table. Peter suddenly felt an overwhelming desire to join them; it seemed to him he belonged among them. Dismissing the feeling as tiredness, he stepped forward towards a semicircle bar, which stood directly in front of him, with eight leather-covered bar stools made up to look like incinerators, the make-believe flames acting as backrests.

A tall dark, very thin man, sporting a short black beard, stood behind the bar, slowly tapping the fingers of his right hand on the bar counter, completely in time with the beat of the piano player's tune, as the other hand gently caressed his beard.

As Peter took a step further towards the bar, he heard the creak of the door as it slammed shut. It made him turn his head, expecting to see someone who had come in after him; he was mildly surprised to find no one there.

Walking over to the bar, he smiled as he spoke to the barman, 'Hello, where's the loo?'

The man pointed with his long index finger and said, 'Through that passage and second right'. He had a deep voice, with a slight guttural tone to it. Peter followed his directions and very thankfully found the toilet– just in time. He stood over the nearest of the three utensils for a full minute; the relief was life-saving. He looked around the small room for the washing facilities. There it was tucked into a corner, a chipped, cracked, and filthy old butler sink. It looked as though it had not been used for two or three decades. In fact, now that Peter had time to study his surroundings a bit more, even the pans were beyond repair, with urine running through the cracks on to the floor. The old stone tiles beneath his feet had sunk in places and were broken in others, allowing water and urine to mix and lie around in putrid puddles. Matching the front of the pub, the small window above the sink was showing signs of extensive wood rot, and the cracked glass was so dirty that you could not see through. Peter thought if he had tried to open it, it would have probably fallen off its hinges. Moving back into the bar, he was amazed at the contrast. The red carpet that was prevalent throughout the floor was truly magnificent, and the high back chairs were polished and covered in yellow and gold material. The round tables were supported by beautiful ornate legs. As well as little lamps situated at regular intervals around the oak panelled walls, there were also two more hanging from the ceiling, and Peter suddenly realised they were oil lamps.

'How long have you been here?' The voice was soft and quiet with an Irish accent. Peter turned round and nearly collided with a very attractive young girl in her mid-twenties.

'I'm so sorry,' he blustered.

'I didn't know anyone was behind me.'

'Please don't apologise,' she replied.

'I was so eager to see if you were real that I got a bit too close.'

'Sorry?' Peter questioned.

'What did you say?'

'Oh, I see.' She looked at him with a slightly hidden grimace on her lovely face.

'You have just arrived then?'

'Well, yes,' answered Peter.

'I'm looking for somewhere to stay for tonight. I've been on the road for hours.'

'You'll be here longer than that,' the girl interrupted, with a shake of her head.

Peter smiled. 'Is that some sort of proposition?'

'No, it's certainly not,' she sounded slightly indignant.

'You'd better come to the bar. I'll explain the situation to you over a drink. I think you are going to need it after you hear what I have to say.'

Without further ado, she turned on her heel and proceeded to thread her way between the tables. Peter, his mind now doing overtime wondering what it could be that was so important, followed her to the bar, where he sat down on one of the stools. He faced her as he said, 'Look, my name is Peter Doddington. We know each other from somewhere, don't we?'

'I don't think so,' she answered.

Peter knew he had heard her voice before. He also felt it had a very calming effect on him when she spoke.

'Yes, I know we have definitely met before. Your voice is so familiar to me!'

'Well, I'm sorry, I can't remember. But it's a good chat up line.' The barman came over and placed two glasses of blood red wine on the counter in front of them; he did not speak, just walked away and sat down on a stool and gazed at nothing.

Peter raised his voice directed at him, 'Excuse me, we didn't order these!' The man was either stone deaf or he was being very rude, because he did not move a muscle, just carried on staring ahead.

'Peter! Please don't say anything, red wine is all they serve here.' She sounded very nervous as she spoke, 'My name is Sophia Andrews and I've been here for two months. There are other people here too, and it seems we are all here for a purpose. Yet none of us knows what that purpose is!' She suddenly reached for a tissue and patted Peter's forehead. It had a very soothing effect on him. He couldn't understand why he didn't challenge her actions. It just felt so natural that he didn't feel it necessary to stop her.

A look of complete astonishment appeared on Peter's face as he listened to Sophia's words; he instinctively gazed around him to try to catch someone's eye in order to recruit some sort of support. He immediately noticed several people staring at him from the tables situated around the floor. Their faces looked blank, with no expression at all as to what their thoughts might be. Again, that strange feeling crept over him like a mist, although Sophia was talking; she sounded as if she was walking away from him. Her voice was growing very faint. For some inexplicable reason, he started to panic, and yet at the same time felt at peace with himself. A few of her words were reaching his ears, and this somehow was giving him the motivation to want to hear more of her voice. With a superhuman effort, he forced himself to take notice of what she was saying, gradually regaining his composure.

He began to feel very nervous, slightly apprehensive even, as he turned back to look at Sophia sitting cross-legged on the stool next to him. She was wearing a pair of expensive jeans, beautifully fitted to her long shapely legs and slim waist; a sleeveless yellow top exposed her smooth, slightly tanned skin on her arms and shoulders. Her short black hair was parted to one side, coming down to the left eyebrow, with deep brown eyes, slightly high cheekbones, and nicely proportioned mouth. Peter thought she was a very attractive woman.

He tried to hide the fact that he felt really scared as he spoke.

'I'm sorry, I haven't a clue what you're talking about, Sophia. What do you mean there are other people here? Is it the people sitting out there at the tables?' Before Sophia replied, she reached across the counter and picked up one of the glasses of wine, put it to her lips, took two sips, and then looked directly at Peter as she slowly placed the glass back on to the bar. She picked up a white tissue and proceeded to gently dab at the little beads of perspiration beginning to form on his forehead. She spoke very deliberately.

'As I've just said, I want you to listen without interrupting me, Peter. When I have finished telling you what I know, I will take you to meet some other people in the same predicament as us, OK?'

Peter nodded his head.

'Yes, OK.'

'Well, first of all, I work for one of the large hospitals in Birmingham.' She reached into her bag as she spoke and retrieved a small white hanky, with which she gently dabbed his top lip. She continued, 'I work as an intensive care nurse.'

'About eight weeks ago, I was on my way to Birmingham. I was supposed to be meeting my colleagues there in order to take part in a one-day course the next day. But as it was getting quite late, I decided to stay overnight at this little inn, which was recommended by an old man at the garage, where I stopped to get some fuel. I managed to get a bed for the night, which I found to be very comfortable. I had a very nice meal brought up to my room. As it was then quite late, I decided to get an early night. It must have been around 2.30 a.m. when I was suddenly awakened by the sound of voices outside my door.

'There was a gentle tap, tap, tap on the door. I jumped out of bed feeling a little apprehensive as I opened it. A group of people stood in the passage outside my room. A woman in her early forties spoke for the others. She said, "I'm sorry to disturb you. My name is Jenny Tollbridge. We have something very important to tell you."

'Somewhat taken aback by the sudden intrusion, my first instinct was to treat them as drunken revellers, but then noticed one of the girls crying uncontrollably. She was being held up by a young man with a shock of red hair. Another man stepped forward and put himself in front of the first speaker. He spoke in a low whisper, "Look, my love, we know it's early hours of the morning, but you really need to be informed of what is going on at this inn."

Noting the urgent tone in his voice, I let them in. Still trying to grasp what was happening, I closed the door as the last person came into the room. I could see there were four women and two men. They all stood there just staring at me. I took a step back and sat on the bed. I must have had a very surprised look on my face, because the girl who called herself Jenny said, "Thank you for letting us in. Please don't be frightened." She turned and directed her voice at her friends, "Do you all agree that I tell this lady what it's all about?"

'They murmured their consent, sat on the floor around the bed, and waited for Jenny to start. At that point, I interrupted and told them my name. Frankly, Peter, I was scared. You can imagine all these people bursting into my room at that time of the night, and me on my own!'

Peter frowned, 'Well, it sounds like something out of "Smile, you're on camera"!'

'Yes, I agree, I thought the same thing myself up to that point, I must admit. But as she started to tell me her story, it became even more bizarre. She, like me and the rest of the people in the room, had arrived at this destination through the recommendation of the old man at the garage. What she said next nearly made me pass out with fright.'

'Now, you're beginning to frighten me,' said Peter, going a bit white around the gills.

'Tell me for Christ's sake, Sophia, what did she say? Don't keep me in suspense any longer.'

Sophia looked at Peter and burst into tears, 'She said once we walk through the pub doors, we can never leave! Peter, she is right. I have been here for three weeks. I have tried to go, but there is no way out of here!'

Peter stood up and took hold of Sophia's hands.

'Now, listen to me, you're talking absolute nonsense. I've never heard anything like it in my life. Now, I am going to the main entrance, and then I'm getting out before I go stark staring mad!'

Without further ado, he walked briskly to the door. Peter came to an abrupt halt and looked in amazement when he saw the door was no longer there. He quickly ran his eyes along the walls, hoping to see some kind of exit, but to no avail. He turned towards the bar in slight panic and saw Sophia and the barman staring at him. He shouted across the heads of the people sitting at the tables, 'Excuse me, mate, where's the exit?'

When nobody replied, Peter lost it. He rushed across the floor, grabbed the barman, and proceeded to pull him over the counter. Out of the corner of his eye, he saw Sophia had something held high in her hand as if about to strike him. His immediate reaction was to twist out of the way, but he felt the stab to his right arm. He heard himself cry out in pain, and a voice said, 'Sorry about that, Peter! It's wonderful you're awake! I'm so pleased it woke you up.'

CHAPTER 3

THE AWAKENING

Peter felt weak, his head ached, he could not move his arms, and there was a distinct smell of disinfectant playing with his nostrils.

The person who had spoken to him called out, 'Doctor! Peter Doddington is awake!'

A voice replied, 'All right, Sophia, I'll be there in one minute.' Peter was now fully conscious. He gazed up from his bed at an angel dressed in a nurse's uniform.

'Hello, Peter, you have kept us waiting. It's lovely to see your eyes open at last.' Peter struggled to find his voice.

'Where am I?'

'You are in Queen Elizabeth Hospital, Birmingham.'

'My God, what am I doing here?' Sophia could hear panic in his reply.

'Sh-sh-sh . . . all right, Peter, don't worry. You're doing very well. You had a nasty accident.'

He gazed around him and discovered he was in a single hospital ward. His mind seemed fuzzy, and he struggled to focus on what the nurse was saying to him. Accident! What is she talking about? he thought.

He moved his eyes to the left; his heart quickened its pace as he saw the tubes leading from different parts of his body to monitors around his bed.

Peter found Sophia's eyes, as tears welled up, and rolled down his cheeks.

'Please, Nurse, tell me what happened to me?' His voice came out in a whisper. Sophia dabbed his eyes with a clean white tissue.

'You were involved in a car accident, darling.' Her softly spoken words had an instant calming effect on Peter, as he forced himself to take control of his surroundings.

'I have been talking to you for the last three weeks, trying to wake you up,' continued Sophia, 'and now I have, at last.'

'Was I badly injured? Am I going to be all right? What are all these tubes for?' Peter's mind was racing.

Sophia sat down on the chair by his bed and moved closer to him and quietly said, 'Look, Peter, you are now going to be fine. You were in a bad way when you were bought in. In fact, we nearly lost you a couple of times. But I have been talking to you for weeks, trying to wake you up. Now you are awake. It's just wonderful. You are now going to make a full recovery. The doctors are amazed at the speed of your response to surgery.'

Peter interrupted her in mid-sentence, 'Where have I had surgery?'

Sophia quietly replied, 'You had a very severe fracture of the scull, so an operation was critical, but as I said, it was a great success. Now Peter, your dad wants to speak to you. He's been here since you were brought in.'

David Doddington came over to the bedside and sat down in the chair next to his son, bent over and kissed him on the forehead, clasping both his hands in a firm grip. He spoke quietly,

'Peter, Son, nice to have you back. Don't you ever frighten me again like that! Thank God you're all right now. The doctors say you will make a full recovery, but you've got a long way to go, so you must take it easy.'

'Thanks for coming, Dad.' Peter was having difficulty speaking through the tears streaming down his cheeks. 'I don't know what happened, Dad, I can't remember a thing . . . '

David interrupted, 'You don't have to worry about that, Son, just be patient and let these wonderful doctors and nurses look after you, and concentrate on getting better. You've got a wonderful nurse looking after you. I've got to know her quite well in the last three weeks. She's a lovely girl. She's hardly left your side. That's enough for now, Peter. I think you should get some rest.' He stood up from the chair just as a tall, heavily built man in his fifties approached the bed.

'Hello, Peter! My name's Jeffery Dunstable, I am the one who has been carving you up! And putting you back together again.' As he spoke, he reached out and took hold of Peter's wrist and felt his pulse. While he was talking, he turned to Sophia.

'How long has he been back with us, Nurse?'

'About a couple of hours, Doctor,' replied Sophia.

'You've been asleep for a long time, young man,' said the doctor, 'but I'm pleased to say you are doing very well.'

Peter looked at the doctor, his eyes still misty from the tears.

'Thank you, Doctor. I can't remember anything about it at all.' His voice trailed off as tiredness swept over him, as involuntarily, he closed his eyes and fell into a natural deep sleep.

CHAPTER 4

REGRETS

Shirley Doddington awoke with a start. She glanced over to the other side of the bed where she expected Tony Harman to be lying down. A sigh of relief escaped her lips when she saw he wasn't there. She lay back in a relaxed position, stretching her long legs as far down to the bottom of the bed as she could, at the same time wiggling her toes, enjoying the freedom of being alone in the house. When her mother had offered to take young Jamie and little Josie to the beach for the day, she had jumped at the chance to spend some precious time on her own, having known beforehand that Tony would be away all day.

As she lay there, her eyes gazed around the bedroom. She looked at the wallpaper. Peter hadn't taken kindly to the rose pattern she had chosen, but eventually went along with it when they decorated. Shirley felt very relaxed at the moment. The opportunity to lie in bed and enjoy the peace and quiet didn't present itself very often, so when it did, it was sheer ecstasy. Looking around the bedroom, she let her eyes wander over the décor, coupling each part of the room with memories generated, when she and Peter had started renovating the house—decorating . . . painting . . . working together, sometimes late into the night; together they did everything to get the house, just as they wanted it. She still felt that feeling of excitement when Peter had told her they had been granted the mortgage. She vividly remembered them clutching hold of each other and dancing crazily around the room, so much in love and, at that time, absolutely convinced nothing would ever come between them. The thrill of renovating the old place was one of the most satisfying periods together; all the family had helped at different times: Peter's mum and David, his lovely dad. In addition, the contribution of his two brothers, who were both in the building trade, was incalculable.

Shirley closed her eyes. She started to question herself, 'My God, what have I done to my life?' Her thoughts wandered back over the last three years to when the affair started with Tony. Tony Harman, as far as she was concerned, was past his sell-by date. He had proved himself to be an alcoholic since they had been together, and now she was at the end of her tether, fed up with the constant rows and fights that seemed to have become a normal part of their lives. She knew the terrible effect it was having on the kids. But apart from that, she couldn't stop thinking about Peter. She was still very much in love with him. And she had made up her mind—she was going to get him back.

She had known Tony Harman nearly as long as she'd known Peter. He and Peter had been friends whilst attending the same school in Wickford, Essex. Apart from a bit of a gap when Peter was away at university, they had been close friends ever since. Tony had lived on a traveller's site at Dale's Farm near Billericay in Essex with his family at the time. The largest illegally established community set up in Europe, it was started many years ago on a plot of land by a small band of travelling people. Gradually and progressively, it became home to about five hundred travellers as a self-contained community, where drains, electricity supplies, and other essential utilities had been installed. Dwellings were erected, growing slowly into a small village. Basildon District Council was currently in a long ongoing dispute over illegal occupation trying to get them evicted. Shirley had recognised from the very start that he was a serial womaniser, but at the same time very attractive, not in a good-looking sense though; rather, he was plain. A rather large nose made his eyes look too close together. A thick moustache covered his top lip but in the process tended to droop over, nearly covering his mouth. He was very well built but not overweight and about six feet in his socks.

He looked what he was: a lovable rogue, a rough diamond. And as Peter and he had been close friends for years before they met, she really had no choice but to accept him as one of the family. He was always there for both of them over the years whenever needs arose, willing to do everything he could to help. However, no matter what he did, or how he acted, her mother always said there was something odd about him and consequently avoided him whenever she could.

After her marriage she didn't see too much of Peter. He was always off on some project for his firm, but sometimes she was able to accompany him, especially when it was for any length of time. She remembered with a warm feeling what wonderful times they were, just the two of them, getting close together; their bodies joined as one, shutting out all the everyday problems you get with mundane living, melting into each other's arms, committing their undying love for eternity, completely oblivious to the rest of the world. It was at one of those times she fell pregnant. She remembered vividly how overjoyed they both were when it was confirmed she was pregnant and how they both got totally involved in getting the nursery ready for the arrival.

When Jamie was born, she was unable to enjoy that part of her life any more. After that, when Peter was given a commission away, where he was unable to get home on a daily basis, he got Tony, his best friend, to keep an eye on things. Tony began to spend a lot of time at their house when this happened, and inevitably, she and Tony began to bond. Not that she fancied him in that way, it was just the company she enjoyed and the way he made her laugh. On one of these occasions, Tony brought in a takeaway and they enjoyed a couple of bottles of wine together. They talked and giggled their way up the stairs and fell in a heap at the top. Shirley's red dress had slid up above her waist baring her thighs and showing her matching thong; her legs parted as she lay back in a semi-drunken state laughing, with Tony straddled over her. He gazed down at her and immediately became aroused; Shirley stopped laughing when she saw him lean over to kiss her, and she did not stop him. She offered no resistance when he removed her thong and made love to her on the landing floor. They slept together that night in the marital bed.

That was the start of the affair, and because Peter was away so much, the illicit meetings carried on for three years, until the day when Peter came home unexpected and caught them in bed together. The memories of that fateful day came flooding back as she lay there, her eyes filled with red hot tears; she wished with all her heart she could turn the clock back.

It was sheer guilt that stopped her from trying to keep her marriage together, feeling at the time to accept the outcome, painful though it was, after the way all of Peter's family had reacted to the news, especially David, his dad, whom she had grown very fond of, saying he would never speak to her again. When she heard those words coming from his lips, she had felt devastated, for he had become like a substitute father to her. It was the best solution for all concerned. However, like many things when dealing with hindsight, she knew she had made the biggest mistake of her life. She never realised how much she loved Peter until it was too late!

Shirley got out of bed and went straight into the shower. The stinging hot water was painful on her skin, but she stayed there until she was bright pink, as though to punish herself.

Sitting at the dressing table, she gazed into the mirror at her reflection. Looking back at her was an attractive woman of thirty-two, long brown hair, big brown eyes with long natural eyelashes and dark complexion. Her breasts were still prominent, with no sign of sagging yet. There was no excess fat on her waistline; she was pleased with what she was looking at.

Her mobile suddenly invaded her thoughts with Frank Sinatra's rendition of 'Come Fly With Me'; she walked over to the bedside cabinet, picked up the phone, and sat down on the bed.

Her mother sounded breathless. 'Shirley, is that you?'

'Yes, Mum, are the kids all right?'

'Yes, darling, they're OK. It's not them I'm calling about, it's Peter!'

'Why, what's the matter with Peter?'

'I'm afraid he's had a very bad accident, darling.'

Shirley stood up and felt her legs give way beneath her as she collapsed back on to the bed.

'Shirley, Shirley, are you all right?' She could hear her mother shouting down to her through the phone. Putting it back to her ear, she heard herself whisper, 'Mum, tell me he's OK.'

'I don't know how bad he is, pet. I only know what David, your father-in-law, told me. They rang him from British Gas. He dashed down to Birmingham straight away, and he rang me from the new Queen Elizabeth Hospital.

'Mum, I've got to go and see him.' Desperately trying to hold back the tears, she got of the bed and walked over to where she had thrown off her clothes the night before. She quickly got dressed, holding the phone in the crick of her neck. Her mum sounded concerned.

'Shirley, think what you're doing. You're with Tony now. You can't go rushing off to Birmingham. What's Tony going to say?'

'Mum, I don't care what Tony thinks. I've got to find out what happened to him! Give me David's phone number, I'll talk to him.'

'Don't be a silly girl, Shirley. You know that none of the family will ever speak to you again after what happened.'

'Mum . . . I still love Peter.' She could not hold the tears back any longer as she slowly lowered herself to the floor, overcome by a feeling of complete helplessness.

'Yes, darling, don't you think I know that, but you have to calm down. I will find out exactly what happened as soon as I can. David has promised to keep me up to date, and then I'll let you know. Meanwhile, the children can stay with me for a couple of days. Will that be all right?'

Shirley heard herself speaking in a daze,

'Yes, Mum, OK . . . thanks, please let me know as soon as you hear anything!'

'You don't have to say that, dear, you know I will. Now try and think sensibly, don't do anything you might regret later on.'

'I wish you could come over, Mum,' Shirley pleaded.

'Now, you know I won't do that, dear. You know very well that whenever Tony and I are in the same house, it always ends up in an argument. No, darling, I'll see you as usual on Thursday. Meanwhile, as I've said, don't do anything without thinking about it first!'

'All right, Mum, I promise. Bye, I love you too.'

As soon as Shirley cut the conversation with her mother, she pressed the buttons of her ex-father-in-law's house phone. She held the phone in her hand, gazing down at it, her mind racing, hearing her mother's voice ringing in her ears . . . think before you do anything, Shirley! She suddenly turned and threw the mobile across the bedroom without pressing 'send' and rushed out of the room in tears.

CHAPTER 5

THE MAKESHIFT

Anthony Albert Harman was drunk, and he knew he should not be driving his car. He kept telling himself it was only a few miles down the road; not only that, he was a very good driver, wasn't he? He knew what he was doing! If he happened to be speaking to any of his mates about drink driving, he would always maintain that it didn't make any difference to his driving when he'd had a few, his reactions were second to none. And what's more, he really believed it.

It had started to rain mid-afternoon, so he had to pack up work early, as he was working outside on the second lift of a new building.

The whole builders' gang immigrated to the nearest pub, with good intentions of just a quick one; five or six pints later they all went their different ways, and now Tony was on the move. He got into his Ford Escort and shut the door. He had difficulty in getting his seat belt on. Instead of looking for an explanation, he kept pulling at it and cursing when it refused to budge. After about twenty-five seconds, he looked down and realised that the belt was caught in the door. Opening the door, he yanked the belt back inside, still cursing. He then forgot to put it on!

Shirley wouldn't be at home. He knew she went to her mother's on Thursday's, so he would crash out for a couple of hours, and hoped he would be sober when she got back. He didn't want another fight. It seemed to him that that was all they did lately, bicker and pick holes in each other. He was reaching the end of his tether with her constant nagging and she wondering why he was always out drinking! Things had been getting a bit out of hand between them lately, he thought to himself; it seemed to have started about the same time Peter had had his accident. At first he couldn't get to grips with the fact that she was desperate to go and see him, and he couldn't. He still thought the world of Peter. It had hit him quite hard when he found out that he had been involved in a bad accident. After a few harsh words on both sides, he reluctantly agreed she could go and take the kids, but only when Peter's health had improved and he was on the mend. He was still, after all that had happened, his best friend!

Shirley accepted the compromise after she had discussed it with her mother, who strongly advised her that it was the correct thing to do given the situation. Tony arrived back home but misjudged the width of the car as he drove up the lane leading to the driveway a bit too fast. He spun the wheel, trying to avoid one side of a brick wall and misjudged the distance. The nearside wing caught the wall and took half of it down. He cursed out loud, switched off the engine, and got out of the car, slamming the door in temper; the window promptly shattered. He walked up to the front door and fell into the hallway and made a dash for the toilet. Feeling more relaxed after relieving himself, he made straight for the settee and fell on top of the cushions. Within three minutes, his snoring could be heard in the kitchen.

CHAPTER 6

RECUPERATION

Peter looked at his watch, which read 8.30 a.m. Doctor's rounds would begin in about an hour. He knew roughly what time they would reach his ward. He was now very familiar with the routine like the back of his hand, after being a resident for six weeks, not counting the three weeks he was in comatose.

He'd been lying awake thinking about how lucky he was to be alive, and the joy he got when Shirley brought Jamie and Josie in to see him, although Shirley at first asked him if it was all right to bring her in. He remembered how he felt when he answered, 'She's still my little girl.' She'd unceremoniously jumped on to the bed shouting, 'Daddy, Daddy', and buried herself in his arms, her blonde curls covering his face. He couldn't help it; he cried, as he cuddled her to his chest.

He and his ex had not talked much or discussed anything about the recent past. However, he could not help noticing she was very upset and once or twice near to tears. She looked very tired he thought.

Peter's dad had insisted on staying at a nearby hotel until he was back to his old self, and dear old Dad would not take no for an answer. Peter was secretly pleased about it. Since his mother had suddenly passed away two years ago, his father had continued to live in the same four-bedroomed house, with a cleaner coming in twice a week.

He was now fully aware of the facts regarding the accident. A truck had apparently sped round a sharp bend in the road and forced Peter to take evasive action, and he swerved into a ditch and hit a concrete mini bridge that was used as an animal crossing.

He sustained a severe fracture of the skull as he was propelled through the windscreen, as well as damage to both shoulders and arms.

Sophia Andrews, who had been designated as his intensive care nurse, had done her job very well. She not only completed her own shifts but also volunteered to do a lot more. The main reason (although she wouldn't have admitted it to a soul) was because she had grown very fond of Peter over the weeks she had been looking after him, seeing not only to his physical needs, but also to the tremendous support she had given him throughout his ongoing recovery to his mental state. Going into deep moods, although alien to him, was quite normal and indeed expected after the nature of the head injury he had experienced. But Sophia was always there to comfort him in a way that Peter had not come across before. Her patience and understanding of what he was going through never ceased to amaze him, so the inevitable nurse–patient relationship was beginning to develop to such an extent that Peter began to wonder how he was going to cope without her once he was well enough to go home! He knew that it was an overreaction to fall in love with someone whom you have become very dependent upon. Because of their commitment to you, it was to be expected. However, he had already made up his mind, despite that bit of logic, that he wanted her desperately. And before he was signed out, he was going to talk to her about it! They had for some time now been exchanging innuendos, and anyone who happened to be around them whilst she was on duty could not fail to notice the outrageous flirting that went on between them. Every day Peter was getting stronger, and as he did, the more he looked forward as the time drew nearer for Sophia's turn of duty, when he would follow her with his eyes as she went about her chores and dream. She came on duty one morning and he noticed she was nearly an hour late. He was sitting on the chair as she came over to make his bed. As she leant over to strip the sheets away, her blouse rode up her back about six inches, exposing an expanse of her bare skin. It was black and blue. When Peter saw it, he gasped.

'Sophia, what's happened to you?'

She very quickly pushed herself up and straightened her uniform; she blushed as she replied, 'It's nothing, Peter. I slipped down the stairs at home the other day, that's all.'

'Did you get it seen to?' he asked.

'No, of course not,' she countered.

'Why ever not, Sophia?'

She seemed annoyed with him and raised her voice half an octave.

'Because it's nothing to worry about, that's why! And any way, it has got nothing to do with you. So please, Peter, mind your business! I'm your nurse, and you're my patient! Do you understand?'

Peter at that moment knew that something was terribly wrong in Sophia's life.

He got out of the chair and walked over to where she was standing by the window.

Standing directly in front of her, he said, 'Look at me, Sophia.'

She raised her eyes to match his gaze.

'Now listen to me,' he spoke very gently, 'I have become very close to you since I've been here, and I think you feel the same, but for some reason you are holding back and will not accept it. Are you married, Sophia?'

'No,' she answered.

'No, I'm not married, but I sort of live with someone.'

Peter pressed home his advantage.

'Do you love him?'

She grimaced. 'Love him? My God, I hate his guts.'

'Then why not leave him?' He carried on, 'I'm single . . . or will be in the very near future. We could be an item, Sophia, because I think—'

She cut him short, and her dark eyes misted over, 'I cannot, Peter. Another place, another time maybe, but not here, not now, not ever. So please, Peter, leave me alone.' She suddenly turned and ran out of the ward.

As far as Peter was concerned, her actions confirmed his suspicions. He therefore came to the decision that to let it slide and do nothing about it would be not only letting her down but also himself.

Being in a single ward had its drawbacks, like not having the opportunity to engage in chit-chat with other patients and wondering what was going on outside, but then again, it was nice when visitors were able to talk in private. Alternatively, when you felt tired, you could turn over and go to sleep without any interruption.

He was in a private ward, and all the medical bills were going to be taken care of by British Gas insurance as he was at work at the time of the accident.

Peter didn't see Sophia any more that day. His dad came in and spent a few hours talking, and he told him how he felt about Sophia. David said he wasn't at all surprised. After that, as his dad wanted to get an early night, he went back to his hotel and Peter went to sleep. The next morning, Sophia knocked and came into the room; Peter, as always, was pleased to see her.

'Hello, my peach,' he said, 'How's my girl this morning?' He had decided not to mention anything about the conversation the day before.

'Hello, Peter,' she greeted, smiling, 'not bad, thank you.'

'You don't sound too sure about that, Sophia.'

'Oh, I'm all right, Peter. I'm a bit tired and fed up, that's all.'

She moved the chair nearer the bed and sat down, clipped the crocodile on to the end of Peter's finger, and read his pulse rate. As she sat next to him, the smell of her perfume slowly crept over the bed and surrounded his senses. He found himself gazing at her as she proceeded to take his blood pressure. He knew at that moment he was hopelessly in love with her.

Her hair was short and dark, with beautiful brown eyes that seemed to penetrate into your very soul when she gazed at you; her skin was as clear and as soft as a young girl, and had a delicate tan. Peter had admired her lovely figure ever since he had started to feel like a man again.

Sophia finished what she was doing and made a move to get up from the chair. Peter couldn't stop himself; he caught hold of her arm and pulled her on to the bed. She sat down with a bump; and didn't move. Peter knew there was something wrong. She turned to look at him, and that's when Peter noticed the red mark on her right cheekbone.

'What's that on your face, Sophia?'

'It's nothing.'

'It's got to be something. It looks like a bruise to me.'

'Yes, that's exactly what it is,' she answered sharply, 'a bruise! I bumped into the swing door, if you must know! I have told you before, mind your own business! Now, if you don't mind, Peter, I've got work to do.' With that, she quickly got up and walked out of the room.

CHAPTER 7

THE CONFESSION

Rene Staples hung the last piece of wet clothing on the line, arranging the pegs, two to a garment; there was not much there in the first place; after all, she now had only herself to look after.

It used to be a lot different when both Tommy and Shirley were here, she mused. Then, the washing machine was going every other day. Stooping to pick up the washing basket, she stood and gazed across the Essex countryside that rolled out before her eyes. Springtime had always been the most appreciated season for both of them. Now, as Tommy had died two years ago to this very day, she knew they would have been busy seeding and planting together. Turning back towards the house, she walked up to the back entrance and heard the front door chimes sounding, at the same time Shirley's voice shouting through the letter box, 'Mum, are you there?'

'Yes, I'm coming, darling. I was just out in the back garden.'

Shirley greeted her mother with a hug and a peck.

'What were you doing out there, Mum, gardening?'

'No, I was just hanging out some washing. I wanted to try and catch this nice sunny day! Do you want a cup of tea, darling?'

Shirley flopped down on one of the comfortable armchairs.

'Yes, please, Mum, I'm gasping. I haven't had time to get one this morning, I've just dropped the kids off at Jesse's.'

Rene filled the kettle and pushed down the switch. Walking back into the room, she sat in the chair opposite her daughter, leant forward, and took hold of her hands. 'Now, how are things with you, darling?'

'Oh, Mum, what a mess I'm in! Everything's going wrong.' Disengaging her hands, she raised them up in the air in front of her. 'I know! I know! It's my own entire fault. I brought it all on myself.'

'Don't talk like that,' her mother scolded, 'nobody plans these things to happen, Shirley, it's just how life is. There's not a person living on this earth that hasn't wished they could turn the clock back at some time in their lives and start over again, armed with hindsight!'

'Yes, I know that, Mum, but that doesn't help me,' she sniped, as she jumped out of her seat.

'Have you been to see Peter yet?' Rene questioned calmly.

Shirley turned and looked at her mother, for a few seconds, as though wondering whether she should tell her secret thoughts regarding Peter.

'Yes,' she answered as she sat down on the chair once more.

'Yes, I did, I took the kids. Tony said he didn't mind. In fact, he said he would have liked to go himself under different circumstances. The kids were pleased to see him . . . '

Her mother interrupted, 'Did he talk to you?'

'Not really, he was too wrapped up with Jamie and Josie. I tried to start a conversation with him a couple of times, but he didn't seem interested. I gave up in the end. After we had left the ward, Josie suddenly shouted "Granddad! Granddad!" and ran up the passageway to where David was approaching us. He stopped and gave them both a big hug and kiss,' Shirley continued, suddenly tearful.

'Mum, he completely ignored me. I tried to talk to him, but he said bye to the kids and walked on down towards Peter's ward. He

did not even glance my way. David's been like a dad to me, Mum.'
Tears were now beginning to well up in Shirley's eyes.

'Come here, darling.' Rene held her arms out towards Shirley,
who willingly let herself be cuddled by the one person she felt safe
and secure with.

'Sit down, I have something to tell you.' Placing her hands on her
daughter's shoulders, she gently guided her on to the comfortable
chair. She took Shirley's hands and held them tight as she continued,
'I am going to tell you something you have got to keep secret, for now,
all right, my darling?'

'Yes, of course, Mum, you're not ill, are you?'

'No, don't be silly, nothing like that!'

'It's just that David and I have been seeing quite a lot of each
other lately,' she paused. 'Well, for quite some time really.' She
wondered why she was having difficulty looking Shirley in the eyes
while she was talking. Looking up, she continued, 'You know, David,
your father, and I always got on very well together, especially when
I lost your dad, you remember what amazing support he was to all
of us.'

Shirley was staring at her mother quizzically. 'Mum, what are
you trying to say?'

'Well, over the past twelve months, since you and Peter broke
up, David and I have become very close.'

'Mum, are you saying what I think you're saying? You and David,
Peter's dad?' Shirley couldn't quite believe what she was hearing.

She sank back into the chair with an incredulous look on her
face, stunned into silence.

Rene responded loudly, 'Well, you don't have to be so shocked.
We're both adults and single, and despite what some people might
think, we haven't got one foot in the grave yet!'

'I'm sorry, Mum,' Shirley replied. 'It has come as such a surprise.
It's the last thing I would have thought could happen.'

'Well, it has, and I have not been so happy about anything in years, and what's more, Shirley, we don't care what anyone says about it. We have our lives to lead the way we want, and it has nothing to do with . . . '

Jumping back on to her feet, Shirley grabbed her mum and pulled her close, wrapping her arms around her, hugging her tightly as though never to let her go. She whispered in her ear, 'Mum, what are you going on about? I am so pleased for you and David. I am over the moon, Mum!'

Rene was in tears as she gently extracted herself from Shirley's embrace.

'I am so relieved to hear you say that, darling. I've been worrying myself to death wondering how I was going to break the news to you!'

'Oh, Mum!' Shirley exclaimed. 'Why didn't you tell me sooner? How long has it been like this? When did it start?'

The questions tumbled from Shirley's mouth faster than Rene could answer any of them.

She took a step back from her daughter and held up her hands in mock surrender.

'Whoa . . . whoa . . . hold on, Shirley! My darling, don't get so excited, we're not getting married . . . well, not just yet anyway.'

Shirley let out a scream and jumped a foot into the air, covering her mouth with both hands.

'You're getting married! Oh, Mum, that's wonderful! Fantastic news! When will it be, Mum?'

Rene was wiping the tears from her eyes as she answered.

'We've put it off for the time being because of Peter's accident. We were going to announce it to all and sundry at about the time it happened, but for obvious reasons we had to postpone, and also, Shirley, you must promise me you'll say nothing to anybody until we have made it official.'

'Oh,' Shirley moaned, 'why not, Mum?'

'David has his reasons, and we must respect them, OK? He agreed for me to let you know, because I insisted. That's what David's like, as you very well know. He knows how close we are and respects what that means to us, despite the inner pain he suffered over the break-up of your marriage to Peter.'

'All right then, Mum, I'll keep quiet about it, but I hope it won't be too long. And I hope I am going to be chief bridesmaid!'

'No, you will not be chief bridesmaid, young lady!' Rene shook her head.

'Why not?' exclaimed Shirley looking indignant.

'Because, my darling, you are going to give me away.'

'That's great! Mum, I would love to do that! But after I have given you away, you'll come back, won't you?' She laughed; her enthusiasm was bubbling over with excitement now, temporarily allowing her to push her own troubles aside for the moment and relish in the thoughts of the future event, which she knew would bring happiness and contentment back into her mother's life.

'Now, I'm going to have a cup of tea, dear. Do you want one?' She disappeared into the kitchen.

'Yes, please, Mum, but I really need something a bit stronger than that, after all the excitement. It's a pity I'm driving.'

Shirley followed her mother into the kitchen and leant against the door frame with her arms folded, staring at her back, wondering how she was going to take the news she was about to tell her. She decided she would just go for it.

'Mum!'

Rene turned to look at her daughter in response. 'Yes, darling, what is it?'

'Mum, I want Peter back,' she heard herself speak, but it sounded as if it had come from someone else.

'Of course you do, Shirley,' her mother answered, without any surprise on her face at all. 'I've known that since the day you split, I just can't understand why you left it so long to find it out!' She continued in a softer tone, 'How you've stayed with that lout for over a year is more than I can comprehend. Peter is in a different league than him! But I don't honestly know how you're going to achieve the impossible!'

As she talked, she moved towards the lounge with two mugs of tea in her hands. Shirley followed and sat down on one side of the settee, taking one of the mugs and placing it on the table before her.

Rene took a tentative sip of her tea before settling down beside her daughter, and said, 'You must know how much you hurt Peter? When you build up a trust in someone, especially in someone you would literally die for, and that trust is then broken in such a devastating way, the way in which you and Tony broke it, then to tell you the truth, Shirley, I will be very surprised if Peter would ever consider coming back to you.'

Shirley looked very forlorn at hearing her mother's words, although she knew they were true. She did not like hearing them confirmed by anyone else, especially her mother.

'Yes, Mum,' she answered slowly, 'but what about Jamie and Josie? Wouldn't he come back for their sake? You know how he adores them, and I know they're suffering because he's not there. Jamie understands the situation, but Josie thinks he's at work.'

Rene shook her head. 'Darling, you have a lot to learn.' She leant forward as if to emphasise her words. 'If Peter agreed to come back under those conditions, it would be for entirely the wrong reasons, and believe me, it wouldn't last six months.'

She carried on in a subdued voice, noting Shirley's previously buoyant mood changing to one of utter despair as she spoke. Rene carried on.

'And as for the children, well, he takes them out nearly every weekend, so it's not as though they never see him. I hate to say it, my darling, but I think the reason you want him back is more for yourself than for the kids!'

She looked Shirley straight in the eyes as she spoke, 'Am I right?'

Shirley leant forward and buried her face in her mum's lap, and through her sobs, she said, 'Mum, what am I going to do? I love him so much, I didn't realise just how much until he'd gone out of my life.'

Rene laid her hands on her daughter's head and said, 'Don't cry, sweetheart, it seems terrible at the moment, but these things take on a different perspective as time goes by. Take my word for it, it will all be resolved one way or another. It's a very true saying: time is a great healer.'

Shirley stopped crying and lifted her head up from Rene's lap. Her eye make-up had formed little black lines on either side of her cheeks.

'Sorry to be such a pain, Mum.'

'That's what I'm here for, love. I shall be here for you as long as I draw breath. Now go and wash your face, and it's nearly time to pick the kids up.'

'Thanks, Mum,' she replied as she leant over and kissed her. 'I honestly don't know what I'd do if I hadn't got you.'

Shirley had dropped the two children off at her friend Jessi's house, who was having a party for one of her three kids, so she knew by the time she'd picked them up, there would be enough time to get the dinner on the table before Tony got home. She just prayed he was not drunk again. She thought, apart from the abuse he threw at her when he was in that state, she always worried about the effect it would have on the children. They were not used to that kind of behaviour; there was never anything like that with Peter. If ever they had a difference of opinion, they saved it until the kids were tucked up in bed.

Her mother had promised she would keep her informed of Peter's progress, and unless anything unusual happened, she would see her next Thursday.

CHAPTER 8

THE CONFRONTATION

'We had cake and ice cream, Mum,' proclaimed Jamie with glee.

'And we had bunny jelly, Mummy,' chirped in Josie.

'No, we didn't, stupid, that was just the shape of it,' Jamie shouted.

'Mum, he called me stupid.' Shirley felt tired and impatient.

'Shut up, you two, and Jamie, Josie is not stupid.'

'Sorry, Mum,' he apologised.

'Don't apologise to me,' she said sternly, 'it's Josie you should apologise to.'

'Sorry, Jo.'

'That's all right, Jamie.' Then, under her breath, she said, 'You're stupid too!'

'All right, that's enough! We'll be home in five minutes, I want you to run straight indoors, it's raining hard!'

Shirley braked suddenly as she came up to the driveway of the house expecting to drive up on to the forecourt as usual, but the headlights had picked out the rubble left by the collision, and the damaged car whose rear end was also blocking her way in. Jamie jumped out of the car.

'Wow! Mum, look at Tony's car, it's all smashed up!'

Shirley got out of the car.

'Jamie, get inside,' she shouted as she lifted Josie out from her car seat.

'You'll get soaked to the skin.'

Tony opened the front door, letting the bedraggled trio into the house. Shirley instantly noticed he had been drinking, by his red face and bleary eyes. She tried to keep her voice as calm as possible.

'What happened outside then?'

'What do you mean, outside? he replied.

'Oh, come on, Tony, don't treat me like an idiot. You know very well what I'm talking about.'

'Oh that, I had a slight accident, that's all, it's no big deal. So don't start going on about it!'

'I'm not going on about it, I couldn't care less about your precious car, and I want to know who is going to foot the bill for my brick wall that you just demolished.'

Tony shouted after her as she continued walking down the hall into the kitchen, 'It'll come off the insurance, of course, you silly cow.'

'Yes, of course it will, especially when they find out you were drunk at the time it happened! (She heard her mother's voice in her ear, telling her to stay calm, take it easy).

She continued, 'My car is stuck halfway across the path. It can't stay there all night!'

She'd put the dinner on a slow burner before she left to go to her mum's that morning, so everything was ready. Tony had sullenly plonked himself down in front of the telly, as she called for the kids to wash their hands and sit down at the table.

Shirley came out of Josie's bedroom after tucking her up for the night, and came into the lounge. Jamie was reading at the table while

Tony was back in the same armchair. She felt the atmosphere as soon as she walked into the room. She stood by Jamie's chair, staring at the back of Tony's head for a brief moment, before she spoke.

'Tony, would you please do something about moving your car? It's dangerous to leave a vehicle across the pathway like that all night.'

Tony slowly got out of his chair and faced Shirley.

'I have no intention of trying to move the bloody thing tonight. In any case, it probably won't start now, so I'll call the garage in the morning.'

'And how do you propose getting to work in the morning?' she enquired.

'That's easy,' he smirked, 'I'll take yours.'

Shirley couldn't contain it any longer; her eyes flashed venomously at him.

'Oh no, you're not taking my car, over my dead body, that's the only way you're ever getting your hands on it.'

'Yeah . . . well, that can be arranged too,' he replied as he made a move towards her. Jamie had heard enough. Getting up from the table, he positioned himself between his mother and Tony.

'You leave my mum alone,' he shouted bravely at the top of his voice.

Tony advanced towards Jamie with his hand raised in the air.

'Shut up, you little snot, and mind your own business,' and with that, before Shirley could stop him, smacked Jamie hard across the face and sent him sprawling on to his back. Shirley was no different to millions of mothers across the world: anyone causing physical harm to their children, were in danger of committing suicide.

'You bastard,' Shirley clenched both fists and flew at Tony.

Swinging her right arm round in a semicircle, she caught him on the left side of his face, knocking him back with her fist. His head hit the wall with a resounding crack, as he tried to dodge the oncoming blow. For a second or two he was visibly dazed; Shirley grabbed hold of his shirt and pulled herself up close to his face, and with her eyes flashing venom, she said, 'That will teach you to hit my kids, you scumbag! Now get out of my house before I call the police!'

'You fucking bitch! I'll teach you!' He raised his fist as if to strike her just as Shirley turned and faced him.

'Go on then, hit me, show me what a big strong man you are.' Tony stopped in his tracks, surprised at Shirley's courage; he stood over her for a few seconds with his fist raised above her head, and then lowered his arm, and sneered, 'You're not worth it. I'm not going to waste my energy on you and your brat of a kid.'

Jamie had got back off the floor; he was crying as he shouted at Tony, 'I'm going to tell my dad what you did to me, and he'll beat you up.'

'You can tell who you bloody well like, sonny Jim, 'cause I won't be here.' With that, he turned round and headed for the door, but not before he had picked up Shirley's car keys which she had carelessly thrown on the hall table.

Shirley ran after him.

'If you don't give me those keys back, I am going to call the police right now.'

'Call who you like, you slag, they won't get mixed up in a domestic dispute. My name's on the insurance policy as co-driver anyway, so I wouldn't waste your time.'

The car's wheels spun on the wet path as he sped off into the night, leaving a sheet of spray to slowly settle back on to the road.

CHAPTER 9

THE COMMITMENT

Peter watched Sophia as she busied herself with the medical trolley. He had noticed when she arrived this morning that she had a slight limp; he could see she was also doing her best to hide it, which made him all the more suspicious. He got up from his chair and walked over to where she was standing. The door was closed; they were alone. He came up behind her; he felt her tense as he placed his hands gently on her hips.

'Sophia,' he whispered softly in her ear, 'I know there is something going on. We have grown close over the last couple of months, and I know you feel the same as I do, and it's no good denying it. You have told me before you're living with a partner. Well, I think that partner is abusing you!'

'Peter, please, do not get involved with me.'

She was still facing away from him as he threaded his arms completely around her slim waist and nuzzled his face in the crook of her neck.

'Involved? Involved?' He repeated, 'My God, Sophia, I've been involved ever since I woke up and saw you standing over my bed!'

Sophia lifted her hands and clasped them over Peter's.

He felt her lungs fill with air as she took a deep breath and held it for a second.

'Peter, I do feel the same about you. I have tried to suppress it, but I can't any longer. We are not supposed to become involved with our patients. But apart from that,' she suddenly turned round, faced Peter, and continued, 'Brett would kill me and you, if he ever found out I was even looking at another man.'

Tears were now starting to make her cheeks wet. Peter pulled her to him and kissed her full on her mouth; she responded with hidden passion as she clung to him. With an effort, she pushed him away and cried out, 'No, Peter, no! I can't allow this to happen. Brett is a terrible man and doesn't care whom he hurts. He's a well-known drug dealer, he mixes with a lot of undesirable people. I'm frightened for what I know he would do to you, let alone me.'

Peter held Sophia's face in his hands and spoke to her determinedly, 'Now listen to me carefully, my darling, I do not care what he is like, or what he is capable of. I love you, Sophia, and I am going to protect you.' He looked at her. 'He beats you, doesn't he?'

She looked away from him as she answered, 'Yes . . . yes, he does. When he's drunk or when he's just had a fix, he starts an argument with me, and when I answer him back, he hits and kicks me.'

'Why haven't you left him?'

'I'm too scared, Peter, he told me if I ever left him, he would find me wherever I went and kill me. And I believe him, for I know what he is capable of.'

'What about the police then? Why can't we tell them?'

'And tell them what, Peter? The police have been trying to nail him ever since he came out of prison three years ago, for what his defence pledged was accidental manslaughter. He got five years and was out in just under three. He is a very clever man. He has many influential people in his payroll, so is extremely hard to get at. So you see, Peter, I'm a hopeless case, and I've just got to live with it . . . ' she paused, ' . . . or not, it's up to me.'

'No, it's not up to you, it's now up to us. You're not alone any more, Sophia.' Peter spoke with a conviction in his voice that Sophia had not heard spoken before. She began to believe it could happen, that she had actually found someone at last who would love her and help her to escape the utter brutality that she had endured for the past eighteen months, and just maybe find some happiness in her life. She lifted her face up to Peter's.

'Peter, I love you, and if we can spend even a short space of time together whatever happens, it will be worth it.'

She clasped her hands together round the back of his neck and kissed him; they stood there for some time like that until disturbed by a knock on the door.

It was the lady with the dinner trolley; Sophia quickly extracted herself from Peter's embrace. Walking over to the bed, she made a half-hearted attempt to straighten the bed and hoped the dinner lady hadn't noticed how flushed she was. They didn't see the woman give a little grin to herself as she left the room.

Peter quickly joined her by the bed and took hold of her; she immediately melted into his arms. Kissing passionately, they fell on to the bed clinging to each other. Peter's right hand dipped under her skirt and felt the smooth silky skin of her thighs. Feeling the touch of his hand, Sophia reached up and started to remove his shirt, her breath starting to come in little gasps.

Discarding his shirt quickly to one side, Peter opened her blouse and pulled down her bra, exposing her beautifully formed breasts. His mouth closed over her left nipple, as she let out a little moan, which brought Peter back to his senses. Getting back off the bed and pulling Sophia back with him, he cradled her in his arms.

'My God, darling, what are we doing? he said breathlessly. He held her to him tightly; she could feel he was very aroused. He continued, striving to get himself under control.

'Sophia, darling, we can't do this here. Anyone could walk in at any moment.'

'Yes, Peter,' she replied.

'I know I'm sorry, I lost control there. I couldn't help myself.'

'Shhh . . . shhh, don't apologise, sweetheart, it was me that started it!'

Sophia straightened herself up and leant forward, taking Peter's face in her hands and kissing him.

'I'm looking forward to the next time, when we won't be disturbed,' she breathed.

'And I promise you,' Peter answered, 'There will be plenty of those in our lifetime together.' He squeezed her hand as she made her way to the door with a distinct sparkle in her eye.

'I'll see you later,' she said smiling.

CHAPTER 10

DANGEROUS LIAISONS

Brett Carlodo was one of those people that no one, regardless of age, creed, or gender, would knowingly go out of their way to make friends with. He was a compulsive liar, a serial cheat, an abuser of women, and possessed an inbuilt obsession with power.

He started his life in Cyprus, where he was born to an Egyptian father and a Spanish mother. At six months, his father decided to leave for better climes, and left his mother to her own devices, where she had no choice but to sell her body to enable herself and her baby to survive. She died of AIDS when Brett was ten (going on eighteen) years old. Having a family already established in the east end of London for some years, it was duly arranged for him to join them, where, after he left school, he joined one of the family's enterprises. They included drug dealing on quite a large scale, the illegal trafficking of girls from East European countries for the prostitution trade, and the counterfeiting of all sorts of commodities, from DVDs to jewellery and films. Over the next ten years, because of his obvious ability to intimidate people and possessing a natural evil streak, he very quickly progressed through the ranks to become one of the most feared criminal operators in Birmingham and London, all under the legitimate business name of 'Gold Star Enterprises'.

Brett eased his large frame out of the rear door of the limousine; his weight had topped over twenty stone the last time he checked. That was about a week ago; sometimes he had difficulty getting enough air into his lungs. He knew secretly that he was a classic heart attack suspect, but one of his favourite hobbies was eating. The other was women. He had no trouble in acquiring the food he liked, and he certainly had his first pick of the beautiful assortment of East European girls, as they came through the back door.

The early rays of the spring sunshine were peeping through the clouds. It was 7 a.m. on Friday the eighth of April. After spending three days setting up some important deals, he just had one more bit of business to attend to. Then he would be dropping in to his London toy factory. He should be back in Birmingham by 11.30 a.m. He started the short walk to the building that stood in front of him. He was already starting to sweat profusely, making his completely bald head glisten like the surface of a still village pond. Despite his obvious weight problem, he moved with surprising agility. Walking up to the big double doors of the warehouse, followed by four young beefy-looking men, one of them stepped forward and promptly opened a side door. Brett stepped through to the interior with his entourage in tow.

Although the warehouse was of significant proportions, it seemed much smaller on the inside. Every conceivable space was used with the utmost detailed planning. Cardboard boxes of all shapes and sizes were neatly placed on pallets and stacked up to the roof, arranged so that corridors ran in uniformly down to the end of the building. If anyone had bothered to look and expected to find anything illegal in those boxes, they would have been solely disappointed. They were all full of toys, from steam engines to Barbie dolls, all part of the intricate measures Brett took to safeguard his security.

One of the corridors ended abruptly, revealing a room arranged as an office.

Three other men in dark suits were sitting in chairs facing a large desk. As Brett and his men entered, they all got to their feet. One of them was the warehouse manager; the other one was a regular customer, who, Brett noticed, had a companion with him. Brett noted mentally that he had not seen the man before. It made him nervous. They all immediately displayed false smiles. The customer offered his hand.

'Hello, Mr Carlodo, it's nice seeing you again.'

Brett ignored the hand and pointing to the man who was standing behind him said, 'Who the fuck is this?'

'Oh, he's a friend of mine, and he would like to do some business with you!'

Brett raised his voice.

'You didn't say anything about bringing somebody else up here. Who the hell do you think you are, opening up a bloody great hole in my security?'

'Well, I'm sorry about that, Mr Carlodo. I thought it would be all right. I do know him!'

'Oh, you know him, well, that must make it OK then, I wasn't aware of that!' he said sarcastically.

'Are you my fucking new security officer?'

'Why can't you people stick to the fucking rules?'

His voice was getting louder as he was shouting.

'The security procedures are made for a reason!' His face was now red and about an inch away from the man's nose.

'How the fuck do you think I keep from getting mixed up with the old bill? Aye, aye.' Each time he said aye, he poked the man hard in the chest with his finger.

'Well, I'm sorry for bringing you in extra business. I assumed that's what you wanted. And what's more, I don't like people poking me in the chest.' At that point, anyone who knew Brett Carlodo well, would have vacated the premises at full speed. Because he suddenly took a step back, his face had turned a deep red.

The man was clearly getting nervous with the way Brett was acting. He knew of his reputation when upset!

'Well . . . no, I thought it would be OK!' the man croaked.

'Well, it's not fucking OK, is it?' boomed Brett.

'You've been dealing with me long enough to know, that no one gets to deal without going through the proper procedure. And as for not liking being poked in the chest, maybe you'll like this better.'

His voice was now reaching a crescendo; his face got even redder and bloated as he swung his big fist and caught the man hard on the nose; he fell backwards and landed on the desk screaming. Brett jumped after him and repeatedly smashed his fist into his face, at the same time screaming obscenities at the top of his voice. After a full minute, he suddenly straightened up, his front covered in the man's blood. Looking around him, he held up his broken hand and shouted, 'Look what the bastard has done to my hand.'

He glanced down at the man's dead body.

'Get that piece of shit out of here.'

Then, looking at one of his men, nodding towards the stranger, who was now making tracks towards the exit, he said, 'Look after him.'

With that, he brushed himself down and shoved his way past the others as he made his way to the outside, with his cronies close behind.

The warehouse was an old barn belonging to a working farm, hidden in the depths of the Essex countryside, about ten miles east of Colchester. The owner was more than willing to let it out to Brett for a ridiculous monthly rent, no questions asked!

The limousine with its four occupants sped along the A-12 towards London where Brett had a toy factory in the East End, staffed by East European workers. All were in receipt of the minimum wage. No one was ever heard complaining about it!

Brett and company duly arrived at their destination. He and his first lieutenant, a short stocky man in his mid-thirties, who went by the name of Snouty because of his double broken nose, and had been with the firm since childhood, disappeared into the building while the other two were told to stay by the car. It was now approaching eight thirty.

The interior of the building was drab with bad lighting and poor heating. Rows of benches, each twenty feet in length, placed in orderly rows, where various pieces of machinery, obeyed the instructions of about fifty depressive looking men and girls, seated on uncomfortable wooden chairs. All seemed oblivious to the intrusion as they concentrated on their repetitive chores. A door to the right opened up to reveal about a dozen East European young girls, between the ages of sixteen and twenty-two, mostly brought in from Lithuania, on a promise of work in the UK. Also in attendance were three of Brett's regulars, men who were there to assess the street value of the girls—in other words, how much revenue can be returned on their investment when they are put to work on the streets and brothels. The girls were lined up, felt, and touched all over; some of them were in tears and started to complain, and got a slap round the face for their trouble. Brett selected one particular girl of seventeen or eighteen, strikingly beautiful, about 5' 10" with jet-black hair and a lovely figure. He took hold of her arm and dragged her screaming into an adjoining room, where he closed the door. For the next ten minutes, her cries for help could be plainly heard through the thin partition walls. When the door reopened, Brett emerged, profusely sweating and visibly finding it difficult to breathe. The girl lay naked and still on the filthy mattress in the corner.

'She gave me a hard time, the fucking slut,' he spluttered as he zipped up his trousers. He turned to his buyers. 'You can have this lot at three grand a head if you take them all!'

The men agreed, the deal was done, and the girls were moved to their new respective 'homes'.

Threading their way between the workers, Brett and Snouty entered a room at the back of the building by using special coded formulae. Closing the door behind them, Snouty fumbled for the switch, then pushed a button. The room was bathed in a bright light showing a completely bare, windowless space of no more than ten square feet.

The two men stood side by side against the far end of the room where Brett produced a remote control from his inside pocket and pointed it at the ceiling; a small flap that had been invisible to the eye as it looked like part of the plaster slid open to reveal a tiny red light; he again pointed and pressed twice; there was a soft whirring noise. The whole floor, except for the strip they were standing on, smoothly rolled back to reveal a staircase receding into the depths of a deep cellar.

Brett and his sidekick quickly transcended the stairs and walked along a passage, passing sealed containers that only they knew were full of class 'A' unprocessed drugs of different varieties.

Coming up to another locked door, Brett produced a key and entered the room, leaving his sidekick outside. He was gone no more than three minutes when he emerged carrying a holdall.

Handing it to Snouty, he said, as though he were handing him a used toilet roll, 'There is 1.2 million Sterling in there, payment for the last shipment. You know what to do, so do it. I want you to keep an eye on things here for a while. I'm going back to Birmingham. Any problems, sort them out, all right?'

Snouty nodded. 'Don't worry, boss, you know I don't have problems.' He stood outside and raised his hand in salute as the car pulled away at speed, heading for Birmingham.

CHAPTER 11

THE ESCAPE

Peter leant back and nestled into the comfortable folds of the armchair, positioned just inside the door of the consultant's room. Mr Jeffery Dunstable had called him in to tell him what he already knew, like, he had suffered a major head trauma, as a direct result of the accident. And he was now being released, but he would have to take the medication prescribed to him for about another six months or so, or at least until his next review date. The consultant surgeon looked up from Peter's notes that lay before him, and smiled.

'Peter, I have to congratulate you on a remarkable recovery. It's only been a matter of ten weeks since your accident, and given the severity of the damage to your cranium, do consider yourself a very lucky man!'

Peter smiled back at the man, who he was sure, had saved his life.

'On the contrary, Doctor, I don't think luck comes into the equation, it was your skill, the absolute care and attention from your dedicated team, especially the intensive care nurses. To all of you, I shall be eternally grateful.'

The surgeon stood up and stretched out his hand, which Peter took and shook warmly with a firm grip.

'Well, thank you for that, it's always nice to hear. Now I expect you will want to go and gather your stuff together, so I'll say goodbye and good luck.'

On his way back to the ward, Peter passed the reception desk; Sophia was standing talking to one of her colleagues. He touched her arm as he said, 'Sorry to interrupt, Sophia, but can I have a word?' He heard her apologise as he walked on and knew she would follow him into the room.

'Sophia, sit down on the bed, we need to talk.'

Letting herself be guided by his words, Sophia whispered as she sat down, 'I know, Peter, I have been thinking about us, and the more I think, the worse it gets. We don't stand a chance against Brett. When he finds out what I've done, he will hunt us down, no matter where we hide, and when he does, Peter, he will kill us both!'

'That is exactly why we have to talk,' Peter answered calmly. 'In order to organise properly, because, my darling, I know what you're going to say: you don't want to risk anything happening to me! Am I right?'

Sophia reached out and took hold of Peter's hand. 'Yes, you are, my love, but if you knew Brett like I do, you would know I'm right!'

Peter now took control as he explained to Sophia, 'I've spoken to my father this morning and put him in the complete picture . . . he knows everything and has agreed to do all he can to help us.'

He continued, 'We are leaving here in about an hour, and you are not to tell anyone you're going, you understand? No one at all. My dad's driving us to a property he owns near Saffron-Walden in Essex. It will be completely safe there, and we can stay for as long as we like or until Brett has given up on us.'

'But, Peter,' she spluttered, 'I can't just disappear like that, what about giving in my notice at the hospital? And what about my clothes and stuff at home?'

Peter silenced her by holding up his hands in front of him.

'No, Sophia, this is the only way it can be done. If we are to achieve any kind of success over that mad bastard, we've got to outplay him and make our move before he knows you've even gone, do you agree with me?' He looked deep into her eyes, as he continued, 'Sophia, knowing what he's capable of, don't you see it's the only way it can be done?'

Sophia put her arms around his neck and kissed him lovingly before she said, 'Darling, I am so happy I met you. My life has suddenly taken on a new beginning. Whatever you decide is best, I will go along with it!'

They both stood up and merged into each other's arms, just hugging, enjoying the sheer pleasure of the feeling of closeness to each other. They stood like that for a full minute. Just as they parted, Peter's father came through the door.

'Come on, you two, no time to waste, let's get on the road out of here!'

Without either of them responding audibly, Sophia and Peter followed David to the car that he'd left parked outside the front entrance of the hospital.

Peter opened the rear door of the car for Sophia and stood while she entered and made herself comfortable. Shutting the door, he went around to the other side and got in beside her.

'You don't mind if I sit in the back, do you, Dad?'

His dad grinned at Peter through the driving mirror.

'I wouldn't have expected you to do anything else, Son. By the way, I've just got to nip back to the hotel to pick up my things and pay the bill. It shouldn't take long, and then we'll be on our way.' David held up his hand in acknowledgement as a black limousine stopped to let him through the hospital exit gates.

'What hotel are you staying at?' enquired Sophia.

'The Holiday Inn Hotel, Smallbrook Queensway,' answered David.

'Oh yes, David, I know that one,' she replied, 'it's a lovely place.'

'Yes,' joined in Peter, 'but it tends to be rather expensive.'

David pulled up at the red traffic lights.

'Yes, Peter, but you get what you pay for in this world.'

'Can't argue with that, Dad,' he replied.

'Here we are,' said David as he pulled into the hotel car park and turned off the engine.

David slotted his door card into the lock and entered his hotel room, followed by Sophia and his son.

'Right,' he turned to Sophia, 'sit yourself down, my dear, I won't be long.'

Sophia sat down on the bed and snuggled up next to Peter, catching hold of his hand and giving it an affectionate squeeze.

'Are you all right, sweetheart?' he said as he gave her a little peck on the cheek.

'Yes, Peter, I'm a bit nervous, I'm sure I'll feel better once I'm out of Birmingham.'

'Of course, you will, my love.' Peter pulled her a bit closer to him. 'I promise you, nothing is going to happen to you or me.'

He was interrupted by Sophia's mobile; Sophia visibly jumped. She reached for her handbag, but Peter got there before her. He pulled it out and looked at the screen.

'It's Brett,' he said, shoving it back in the bag.

'If we switch it off, he'll know you've heard it, so we'll just ignore it, OK?'

Sophia's face had turned white. Peter held on to her and whispered, 'I know what you're thinking, but I'm here to look after you now.'

David stopped packing his bags and fished out his mobile, as it started ringing. Turning his back, he answered, 'Hello, I beg your pardon. Sorry, could you repeat that? It's a terrible line. Yes, speaking! Yes, of course, I know her!' Peter was listening with interest, but did not want to appear as though he was eavesdropping, so was looking away from his dad.

Suddenly, David shouted out loud, 'What!' He sat down on the other side of the bed and carried on, 'Oh my God, when was this?' A pause and then he continued, 'OK, how is she?' Another pause. 'Yes, where?' David repeated.

'Basildon University Hospital, yes, I know where that is. I'll leave right away, thank you, goodbye.'

Looking at Peter, he said, 'Rene, Shirley's mum has had a stroke.' He was shaking as he put the phone back in his pocket.

Peter stared at his father in amazement as he said, 'Well, I'm sorry to hear that, Dad. I like Rene, but don't you think you're overreacting a bit?'

David was becoming very agitated as he answered brusquely, 'You don't understand, Peter, and I haven't got time to explain now, but believe me, this is of the utmost importance to me! I am going to have to leave you two here, because it's imperative that I go straight to the hospital.' He continued speaking as he gathered his stuff together.

'Stay at this hotel, no one knows you're here, so it's safe. Stay put until I phone you and let you know when I'm coming to get you, OK?'

He moved towards the door.

'Goodbye, kids, you'll both understand later.' And with that, he was gone. After they had got over their surprise at David's seemingly strange behaviour, Sophia looked at David, 'Who's Rene?'

'My mother-in-law,' answered David. 'She is a lovely lady.'

'What about her daughter?'

'What do you mean?'

'Well, is she lovely too?'

'What!' he exclaimed.

Sophia straight away wished she hadn't said that.

'I'm sorry, David, I didn't mean that!'

David smiled and patted her gently on the nose.

'Yes, you did, and to answer your question, yes, she is lovely.

She was lovely when I met her, she was lovely to look at, and she was lovely to be with. Why else would I have married her?'

Sophia looked down as she said, 'Are you still in love with her, David?'

'Where is all this leading to, Sophia?'

Sophia looked up into David's eyes. She held her gaze for a few seconds before answering, 'David . . . I have got to be sure, secure in my mind that you are not going to have second thoughts about us after a period of time. I have experienced so many let-downs in my life that now I'm afraid I have become a bit on the cynical side. And, Peter, I want this relationship so much to work, I have never felt this way about anyone in my life before. My father was a paedophile. He was sent to prison for ten years when I was six years' old. My mother introduced me to a host of uncles over the years, until she died when I was fourteen.'

David leant forward and kissed her on the lips.

'I am so sorry, Sophia, I didn't realise.'

'Of course you didn't, Peter, how could you? I've never told anyone about my life before.' Peter held her close.

'I'm not in love with Shirley,' he said. 'She destroyed my love. It died, as far as she was concerned, over a year ago. I'm in love with you, Sophia, and I always will be!'

David spent the next two hours relating to Sophia, more or less, his life story, right up to the time he first set eyes on her, after which they went to bed and made love to each other for the first time, then ended up in the shower together and made love again before ordering dinner, which was brought up to their room.

CHAPTER 12

THE DISCOVERY

B rett was in a very bad mood, sitting in the back of the car that was now completely stationary, gridlocked on the M1, because of an overturned lorry several junctions ahead of him.

He swore to himself; a journey that should take two and a half hours was now creeping into its third hour, with no sign of any movement becoming likely in the very near future.

Opening a panel in the floor, he pushed a button and activated the television; the fifteen-inch screen illuminated immediately. He selected the travel channel, sat back, and watched in anticipation. The news presenter quickly confirmed what he had heard on the radio earlier. With an added piece of good information, the lorry had now been removed and all lanes were now beginning to move, albeit slowly. Brett leant forward in his seat and tapped the driver on the shoulder. 'When we get to Birmingham, go straight to the Queen Elizabeth Hospital to the A&E department.' The man nodded without turning his head. Brett settled back in the seat; his right hand was now swollen and turning various shades of purple, throbbing, and the pain becoming unbearable.

As David's car was leaving the hospital grounds, with Peter and Sophia tucked up on the back seat, Brett's limousine gave way to him before entering. David acknowledged with a wave of his hand.

After receiving the services of the excellent A&E department, Brett told the driver to take him home.

Brett Carlodo possessed no less than three of them, Birmingham, Alicante, and Florida, but this one was his base: a sumptuous six-bedroomed detached house, built to his own specifications, standing in its own grounds on the edge of Moseley Golf Course in Cold Bath Road. He also owned the two-bedroomed flat that was occupied by Sophia Reynolds (rent-free) in Highbury Road, near Kings Heath Park.

When Brett arrived, he immediately went to the library, sitting down behind a heavy oak desk. This was one of his favourite rooms, surrounded by books of every description. He was an avid reader. One of his staff (there were four of them in permanent residence) had brought him in his usual treble Whiskey and Ginger ale, which he now gulped down in two swallows.

Muttering to himself, 'that's better', he reached for the phone and dialled Sophia's mobile. It made the connection immediately but continued ringing until the usual interruption of 'please leave a message'. Visibly annoyed, he redialled and then slammed the phone down hard on to the desk when he received the same response. In the eighteen months of their relationship, there had never been a time when she had not answered the phone. He knew something was not right; he felt the feeling of uncertainty starting to develop somewhere deep within himself. It made him very angry. After all the money he had spent on her, furniture for the flat, jewellery, clothes, her car! All right, he reasoned, he had hit her a few times, but the bitch deserved it! He hated that feeling, and good reason why he should, he was losing control. His anger started to show by the colour of his face;

it was slowly turning a darker shade of red. He pressed a button on his desk that summoned Phil 'The Pill' Bosworth (so named because he was a confirmed hypochondriac) to the library. Phil had been on Brett's payroll for years; he was a trusted member of the inner circle but never took liberties (not in front of the 'boss' anyway); he knew his place. Phil entered the room almost immediately and stood by the desk.

'Yes, boss?'

Brett waved him into a chair.

'Phil, I've got a little job for you,' he said, whilst writing down Sophia's address.

'You know where that is?' he asked, passing the paper across the desk.

'Yes boss, that's down by the park.'

'You've got it, Phil, I want you to go down there and find the girl who lives there, all right?'

'Sure thing, boss,' he answered, 'what do you want me to do with her?'

Brett stood up from the desk and leant forward supported by his hands. Through gritted teeth, he hissed, 'Bring her back here, and drag her back by her fucking hair if you have to.'

As Phil was going out the door, Brett shouted an afterthought, 'Take a couple of the boys with you.'

CHAPTER 13

THE CHASE

David felt really terrible about having to leave his son and Sophia alone in the hotel under the potentially dangerous circumstances. He realised it must have looked a bit strange to Peter, seeing his father acting so odd! However, he knew he would understand when he eventually got to know about him and Rene. The M1 was as busy as ever as he joined the long line heading towards London. As usual, because he was in a hurry, everyone was getting in his way. But he knew that was a fallacy. Having broken every rule in the highway code, David arrived at Basildon Hospital at two thirty in the afternoon, just two hours and twenty minutes after he left the hotel in Birmingham. Finding a parking space proved to be another hurdle he had to overcome, which he eventually did by moving into a space being vacated by another car. He was just getting ready to congratulate himself when he saw, staring in front of him on the wall, the familiar sign of the disabled badge. Under the circumstances, he forgave himself, switched off the engine, and locked the car as he hurriedly made his way to A&E.

He arrived at the reception desk slightly out of breath, which prompted the receptionist to enquire whether he was OK. David ignored the question.

'Please, could you tell me the name of the ward they have taken Rene Staples, I think she had a stroke.'

'Just a minute, sir, and I'll find out for you,' the girl replied.

Consulting the screen in front of her, she proceeded to tap out the appropriate question on the keypad; the answer came back in less than a second.

'There you are, sir, you'll find her in Lister Ward, that's the Jubilee Wing on level four. You'll find the lifts down at the end of the corridor, turn left and the lifts are on your right.' David thanked her and made his way to the lifts as fast as he could. He was pleased he was the only one waiting; stepping inside, he pressed the button that would take him to level four. As the doors opened, he came face-to-face with Shirley. They both stopped dead in their tracks and stood there staring at each other for a few seconds, as though waiting for the first to make a move. Shirley was the first to give way to her feelings. She burst into tears. David, who had become very close to her during her marriage to his son, stepped forward without a moment's hesitation and drew her into his arms.

'Oh, Shirley, my darling, come here,' he said.

'I'm so sorry, David, for causing so much trouble for everyone.' Her sobs were coming from deep within her, as though they had been waiting to get out for a very long time. David held on to her until her body had stopped shaking and she was a lot calmer. 'How's your mum, Shirley?'

She looked up at David.

'She's not too bad, she's sleeping now, so I thought I'd try and grab a cup of coffee.'

David stepped back and said, 'All right, darling, dry your eyes . . . ' He passed her a clean white hanky. 'and have a break, I'll go in with your mother now, I'll see you later, all right?' Patting her affectionately on the arm, as she stepped into the lift, he proceeded in the direction of the Jubilee Wing and Lister Ward. Pressing the security entrance button, he announced his name and who he was intending to visit. The door opened and closed behind him. The reception was in front of him.

The nurse looked up from what she was doing and asked, 'Can I help you?'

'Yes, I'm looking for Rene Staples.'

She called over to one of her colleagues, 'Jenny, would you show this gentleman to Rene Staples please?'

Jenny moved towards David. 'If you would like to follow me, sir.'

David duly obliged and found himself standing by Rene's bed. She looked peaceful and beautiful, he thought, as he stood gazing at her.

Drawing up the chair, he sat down and took hold of her hand, held it to his face, and kissed her fingers lovingly. He could see that the left side of her face had dropped noticeably. Although he had always considered himself to be a strong person, able to control his emotions to a certain degree, he was now finding it extremely difficult, sitting with her, and not knowing if she was going to recover.

It was five o'clock when Rene opened her eyes and saw David sitting there. She immediately tried to speak, but the sound would not come out, but he saw the words reflected in her eyes as clearly as if she had spoken them. Shirley was sitting on the other side of Rene's bed with a worried look on her face. David spoke softly as he saw Rene's lips start to move.

'Don't try to speak, my love, you've got to rest. I'll be here with you now, I'm not going anywhere,' he paused, 'not now, not ever!'

Shirley gave David a loving glance; she felt an overwhelming sense of relief that someone as strong and caring as David had become one of the most important people in her mother's life! After about an hour or so, Rene dozed off again.

Shirley was trying to pluck up the courage to ask David some questions she desperately wanted the answers to. After a few more minutes, she broke the silence and casually queried, 'How's Peter, David?' He took his eyes away from Rene and focused on Shirley.

'Yes, he's making progress every day,' he ventured. Shirley pressed home her advantage.

'Has he been discharged yet?' David looked away as he told her a deliberate lie.

'No, no, not yet, he's OK! But they won't be discharging him yet awhile!' David neatly changed the subject. 'Shirley, how did you manage to get here today? Has Tony brought your car back?'

'No, he hasn't,' fumed Shirley. 'I haven't seen Tony since he walked out.' Then after a pause, she asked, 'How did you know Tony had taken my car?'

'It's all right, darling. Your mum told me what happened. That man has a lot to answer for in my book.'

He continued, 'Shirley, why don't you go and get something to eat, then I'll go when you come back.'

Shirley smiled.

'Actually I am pretty hungry, David, are you sure you don't mind?'

'Of course not, you go ahead.' With that, Shirley got up and disappeared in the direction of the canteen. She quickly found a table in the corner under a window and settled down to a plate of spaghetti bolognaise. She was just about to take the first spoonful when the sound of her mobile interrupted the move in mid-air. She quickly replaced the spoon on the plate and picked up the offender.

'Hello! Shirley?' The voice was quiet, but Shirley froze.

'What the hell do you want?' she yelled down the phone.

'Shirley, please listen to me, I am not drunk. I've stopped drinking now.'

'And you expect me to believe that!' she screamed.

'Where's my bloody car?'

'That's what I'm ringing about, among other things,' he answered.

Shirley became suddenly guarded.

'What do you mean other things?' Tony became hesitant.

'Well, you know . . . us . . . and Josie!'

Shirley exploded, 'Tony, there is no us, and as far as Josie is concerned, you are not even on the birth certificate as her father!'

Tony interrupted, 'Now don't start going down that road, Shirley, you know she is mine. If you insist on adopting that vengeful attitude, I'll get a DNA to prove she is mine!'

Shirley noticed people were looking at her slightly amused. She realised she was shouting. In a much calmer voice, she said, 'All right then, but do you intend helping with the expense of her upbringing?'

Without any hesitation, Tony was jubilant.

'Shirley, I love that little girl. She is the one thing that I have managed to get right in my life, so yes, I will make sure she gets everything her little heart desires.'

Shirley was repentant.

'All right, Tony, we'll talk about it when you bring my car back.'

Tony's enthusiasm sounded in his voice.

'Where are you now? If you're at home, I can bring it back now and you can run me back home.'

Shirley lowered her voice a shade.

'No, you can't. At the moment I'm in Basildon Hospital.'

Surprise was in his tone.

'Basildon Hospital!' he repeated, 'What are you doing there?'

'My mum's had a stroke.'

'What? Oh my God, Shirley, I am so sorry, I didn't know! How is she?'

'She doesn't look too bad, but they've got to run a load of tests yet, so we won't know until they get the results back.'

Shirley, feeling the need to get back to her mother, continued, 'Look, Tony, bring the car back tomorrow morning about ten. We'll talk then. I've got to go now.'

Tony readily agreed as they said their goodbyes.

Shirley finished her meal and hurried back to her mum's side. She was asleep, and so was David. She sat down on the chair and made a scraping noise as the chair moved towards the bed. David opened his eyes.

'Sorry, David,' she whispered, 'I didn't mean to wake you.'

'That's all right, Shirley,' he replied rubbing his eyes, 'I was just dozing.'

'You must be shattered driving all that way,' she said.

He smiled. 'Yes, I must admit I do feel a bit that way. It's old age creeping up on me, Shirley.'

'Don't talk like that, David, there's nothing old about you at all.' Shirley laughed. David was pleased to see her in a better mood.

'Did you enjoy your meal?'

'Yes, it was quite nice, although a bit cold.'

After a short lapse in the conversation, she decided to tell David about the phone call from Tony and that he had promised to bring the car back tomorrow. David seemed to sink into deep thought after that piece of news. He did not make any comment other than to ask Shirley if she would mind him being there when Tony arrived. She assured him she had no problem with that.

CHAPTER 14

****DANGEROUS GOSSIP

P hil (the Pill) gathered two of Brett's team and briefed them on the job in hand. Reggie and Harry were both already petty criminals when they found themselves owing favours to the organisation, which meant they had no choice (when asked by the firm to do some work on their behalf) but to ask how high they should jump, at the same time guarantee total commitment or face the consequences! So now, they just followed orders without question whatever it was, or whoever it involved.

Phil swung the car into Highbury Road and slowed to a crawl noting the house numbers. Number 36a came up on the left-hand side of the road. He parked the car. They all made their way up two flights of stone steps. Phil hammered on the door. He waited about ten seconds before he pulled the key Brett had handed him, out of his pocket and entered Sophia's flat.

Closing the door behind them, he gestured to Harry to look in the first bedroom, while the two of them carried on into the spacious lounge; it was obvious a woman lived here; there were pink curtains and a matching profusion of cushions scattered round the black leather sofa and two comfortable armchairs. A thick pile white carpet covered the floor and a forty-two-inch flat-screen television was sunk into the far wall. A heavy marble top coffee table graced the centre of the room. A few gossip magazines were lying around.

Phil told Reggie to go and look in the other bedroom, while he helped himself to a double scotch. (He liked the thrill of taking a chance now and again.)

Harry and Reggie both came into the room together and caught Phil sinking the last dregs of the scotch down his throat. Reggie laughed out loud and joked.

'If the boss could see you now, Phil, you'd be for the high jump!' Reggie never saw the move coming. Phil swung his arm round and hit him on the side of the head, the glass still in his hand. Blood immediately spurted from the open wound and quickly spread round the carpet, adding even more colour to the surroundings. Phil was, among other things, a schizophrenic, who should have been detained many years hence, but somehow he had always managed to slip the net.

He did not raise his voice when he replied to the bleeding man. He just said, 'If you tell him, Reggie, that's just a little taste you're going to get before I kill you! Now Harry and me are going to the hospital, we'll pick you up in a couple of hours. Make sure this mess is cleared up before then, all right?'

Reggie, holding a large handkerchief over the gash on the side of his face, desperately trying to stop the bleeding, nodded as they left the flat. They arrived at the Queen Elizabeth Hospital and stopped at the reception desk. The woman sitting behind asked if she could be of assistance.

'Yes, I'm looking for Nurse Andrews, could you tell me if she's left yet?'

The receptionist looked directly into his eyes and queried, 'And you are?'

'I'm just a friend, love.'

'I see, and your name, sir?'

Phil was becoming visibly agitated.

'Look, girl, don't mess me about, I just want to know if the bloody nurse has left yet?' The receptionist quite rightly took offence to his tone.

'We do not tolerate any kind of abuse here, sir, and if you carry on using that kind of language, I'll have no option but to call security!'

Phil turned and walked away, muttering under his breath. Fuck you too, lady.' Harry noticed a sign giving directions to the restaurant.

'Could we grab a cup of coffee, Phil? he asked. 'I'm starving!'

'Yes, all right,' Phil replied.

'I could do with one myself.'

Being mid-afternoon, it was pretty quiet, with just a scattering of visitors and hospital staff. The two men sat down to meat pudding and veg. About halfway through, three women dressed in smocks sat down at an adjacent table. They were chatting and giggling as they started to drink their tea. One of the women was saying something about 'when men and women work together, things start to happen.' Phil was listening to the chatter, wishing they would clear off. Then he heard one of them giggle.

'It goes on here quite a lot, you know, between the doctors and nurses!'

'Yes, I know, even between nurses and patients sometimes,' the third one chimed in.

'I don't know about that, I wouldn't have thought so,' said the first.

The second woman finished the scoring by adding, 'Well, the other day I was doing the dinners, I walked into the ward and that nurse Sophia was in a clinch with Peter, you know, the one who had the car crash.' They all laughed out loud at the revelation as they got up from the table and went back to work. Phil had taken the information on board. He wondered if they had been talking about the boss's girlfriend. He decided he would have to make some discreet enquiries.

Phil moved his chair back from the table.

'Have you finished, Harry?' he asked.

'Just about,' replied Harry.

'I'll only be a second or two.'

'Well, no rush,' said Phil, 'you wait here a minute, I've got something to do.' Phil disappeared hurriedly out the door and saw the three women further up the corridor in front of him. Quickening his pace, he soon caught up with them. He was smiling as he said, 'Excuse me, ladies, I couldn't help overhearing your conversation just now. I think you were talking about a friend of mine in the restaurant. I don't know what ward he's in. His name is Peter.

One of the women interrupted, 'Oh, I know who you're talking about, Peter Doddington.

Phil reacted swiftly.

'Yes, that's the one. What ward is he in?'

'You're too late, I'm afraid,' was the reply, 'he's been discharged.'

Phil decided to push his luck.

'Any of you know where I could find Sophia Andrews?'

One of the women was becoming suspicious.

'What do you want to know about Nurse Andrews for?'

Phil thought he had outstayed his welcome.

'Thanks, ladies,' he shouted as he exited down the way he had come. Joining up with Harry, they made a quick return to the car and headed towards Cold Bath Road, stopping on the way to pick up the forlorn-looking Reggie. Phil knew Brett would be pleased with the information he had managed to glean from the dinner ladies.

Brett was pleased with Phil's detective work. He was like a cat that had not been booted out of the house for once.

Brett was on the phone immediately to one of his many contacts. It picked up straight away.

'Yes, Simon Rafferty,' the voice was firm and crisp.

'Simon, my boy, how are you?'

'Oh, hello, Brett, what do you want this time?'

'Nice of you to ask how I am, Simon. Yes, I'm very well and how are you? he asked sarcastically.

'Cut the crap, Brett, tell me what you want. Just because you've got something over me doesn't mean I have to put up with your warped sense of humour too!'

Brett's voice suddenly became as cold and unfeeling, as a piece of ice.

'You'll put up with whatever I want you to put up with, Simon. I want you to check out a man by the name of Peter Doddington. Find out as much information as is humanly possible, OK, Simon? Let me know as soon as possible.'

Simon lowered his voice, 'I'll do what I can.'

Brett's tone was chilling. 'Yes, Simon, I know you will.'

Simon Rafferty, equal partner in the law firm of Rafferty, Rafferty and Partners, was very successful in their speciality of criminal law. Happily married with two little girls, two years ago on a stupid stag do in honour of his best friend's wedding, he had had too much to drink and ended the night fully recorded on CD with two eighteen-year-old girls beside him in the nude. Brett had caught him literally with his trousers round his ankles. He had him just where he wanted him . . . dangling on a thin piece of string! With his wife, his kids, and his livelihood relying on it holding up to Brett's whims, he moved quickly to gather the information as soon as he put the phone down on Brett, because he knew Brett would get the utmost sadistic pleasure in exposing him to his wife and colleagues, the first time that he, Simon, couldn't come up with his requests.

Brett Carlodo received a package, from Simon Rafferty, in the next morning's post. It contained all the information he had asked for relating to Peter's personal details:, his marital address, date of birth, marriage date, birth dates of his children, what his job was—even his financial situation—details of his marriage break–up, his recent accident, and the time he left the hospital. But he was missing one vital piece of information: Where was he now? And was Sophia with him?

He was sure of one thing; they would pay dearly for trying to put one over on him. There was not one person alive that could honestly say they had got the better of Brett Carlodo.

Phil and Harry sat in comfortable armchairs, each with a glass of their favourite alcoholic beverage in their hand. Brett sat opposite, behind his massive, polished solid oak desk. The floor the desk stood on was slightly raised, giving him the misconception of authority and power, which somehow never quite gave him the complete satisfaction he yearned for!

He sat staring at the lines of books which graced three walls of the room. The two other men sat in silence, knowing that to interrupt the boss's train of thought would not be an advisable thing to do.

Five minutes of their respective lives had passed them by, when suddenly, Brett stood his empty glass on a black cork coaster in front of him.

Raising his considerable bulk out of the chair and resting his hands on the desk, he nodded his head in the general direction of his two puppets. His breathing was not so good as he said, 'Right, Phil, this is what I want you to do. Go down to a village called Paglesham in Essex. That's where this bloke . . . Peter Doddington lived, with his . . . wife and kids up to about fifteen months ago. I want you to find out anything . . . you can, OK? He had to keep pausing to take a breath.

'Any information . . . that will give a clue . . . as to where he could be.'

If you see his wife, pose . . . as an insurance investigator . . . acting on behalf of . . . British Gas. She might be dumb enough . . . to fall for that one . . . all right, Phil?'

Phil answered promptly, 'Yes boss, I've got all that.'

'Well, you'd better had, because I need to know . . . where that son of a bitch . . . has taken that slut of a nurse. And I need to know now!'

He raised his voice a full octave.

'Where the fuck does . . . she get off, thinking . . . she can walk out on me, after all the fucking money I've . . . lavished on her.' His face was gradually turning a deeper shade of red as he rampaged on. He now was not necessarily talking to Phil. In fact, for the next few seconds he was completely oblivious to his surroundings.

'I am determined to find . . . that pair of bastards, if it's . . . the last thing I do! And when I do get them back here . . . I shall personally see to it . . . that both of them will . . . wish they had never seen the light of day before I get rid of them!' And with that last explosive outburst, he slammed his uninjured fist down on the top of the desk.

He then sat down heavily back into the chair. His breathing was visibly laboured. Beads of sweat, which had formed on the top of his head and on his forehead, were now running down into his eyes. Pulling a large white linen handkerchief from the right-hand desk drawer, he proceeded to wipe his face, at the same time reaching for his Ventolin pump, in a desperate attempt to get his breath back. Phil got up from his seat and moved closer towards the desk.

'You all right, boss?' he asked, in an unconvincing attempt to sound caring.

'Yes, of course I'm all right,' he spluttered. 'Now go and get that information . . . and keep me informed.'

Phil and Harry left Brett's house with his words still reverberating in their ears. They had estimated that the journey to Paglesham would take them about three hours. It was now ten in the morning, so with no unexpected hold-ups, come one o'clock, they should be there.

Phil woke up, removed his feet from the dashboard, and sat up straight, trying to make out to Harry that he had not been asleep the whole of the trip.

Paglesham was a tiny village, situated next to the River Crouch, just east of Southend-on-Sea. A very nice place to live, thought Phil as he gazed through the window of the car.

'Drive down to the next lane, Harry, and we'll walk back to the house,' he said as he took a small bottle of pills from his pocket and slipped a couple into his mouth. Walking back to the house, Phil could not help admiring the lovely old buildings they passed on the way there. Phil pushed his thumb on to the doorbell button. A usual doorbell sound came from somewhere within. They waited for a response but were not rewarded. Phil and Harry stood looking at each other for a minute. Harry spoke first.

'Are you thinking what I'm thinking, Phil?'

'Yes, Harry, I believe I am,' he replied.

'Creek abode' stood in half an acre, most of it covered in well-kept lawns. Shirley had done her best to keep it that way since Peter left, but she found it hard going. Tony never lifted a finger to help in the garden while he was there.

The demolished brick wall restricted their approach somewhat, so they parked the Land Rover and walked up to the house.

They quickly made their way round to the back. Harry produced a very thin bladed knife. The double glazed kitchen window was in front of him. He slotted the blade into the side of the trim, and with an expert twist sprung the uPVC retainer from its housing. Having removed the other three, the unit was lowered to the ground. Phil climbed in through the open space and opened the back door. Leading the way to the front of the house, Phil went into the lounge to poke around, while Harry stopped to look at an address book on the hall table. After leafing through a few of the pages, he called out to Phil.

'Come here, Phil, I think I've found something.' The call brought Phil scurrying back.

'What yer got, Harry?' he grunted.

'Well look, there's an address here under "Mum", and the telephone number. Do you think it could be that Peter's mum?'

'Yes, I think it might be at that, Harry,' he answered. Another half an hour's searching failed to reveal anything of interest. They left the house as they found it. The double glazed unit was replaced and the retainers sprung into place. Nothing had been disturbed. Or so it seemed!

The journey from Paglesham to Stock took about forty minutes. And once again Phil admired the beautiful Essex countryside of which the village of Stock was a prime example.

Rene's house was a four-bedroomed detached residence, which lay back off the road by two hundred metres and was completely hidden by a forest of fruit trees. Harry and Phil were able to gain entry very easily, having made sure no one was at home. And they found what they were looking for. Lying exactly where Rene had placed it on the table was written on an envelope the name David and underneath a hotel that Phil was very familiar with, the Holiday Inn, with the telephone number.

Having achieved their goal, they moved quickly out of the house and walked back to the car and headed back to Birmingham. The time was 2 p.m.

CHAPTER 15

THE PLAN

Tony Harman was true to his word. He arrived at the house the next morning as promised with Shirley's car cleaned and shiny. Shirley opened the front door and invited him inside.

'Hello Shirley,' he said quietly.

'Go inside, Tony, somebody wants a word.'

Tony glanced at her quizzically. 'Who's that then?'

'It's me, Tony.' The sound of David's voice was the last thing Tony expected to hear; he was visibly surprised.

'Hi, David.' He was doing his best to stay with it. He had not had a drink for three days. 'How are you?'

'I'm very well, thank you, Tony, and you?'

'I'm good.'

David invited him to sit down with a wave of his hand. Shirley came into the room and went to one of the armchairs. Before she could make herself comfortable, David looked at her and nodded. (He had previously arranged to speak to Tony alone.) Shirley took the hint and immediately left the room.

David sat down, wondering how he was going to lay out the plan he had devised, to get Tony sufficiently interested, to be able to make it work!

'Tony,' he started. 'What I am about to tell you must go no further.'

'Both of us are going to put aside, for the time being, the histrionics that will live with us forever!' He paused to clear his throat.

'My son . . . your friend has found himself in a very dangerous situation.'

Tony sat upright with both hands spread on the arms of the chair. 'What do you mean dangerous?'

'Now as I've just said, and I repeat, this conversation remains in this room!'

Tony nodded. 'Yes, of course.'

'As you are probably aware, Shirley has made it clear she wants to get back with Peter.'

Tony again nodded his head. 'Yes, I know.'

'That is going to prove impossible, but she doesn't know it yet!' said David. He carried on. 'You see . . . Peter is in love with someone else.'

'Oh my God!' Tony showed his surprise.

'Exactly,' exclaimed David.

'This is where the danger comes in.'

'Yes,' invited Tony, 'go on.'

'Her ex-boyfriend is a high-profile criminal operator, tied up in every kind of illegal activity you could mention!

'And make no mistake, when he discovers his woman is cheating, he will eliminate both of them without a trace, but to do that, he first has to find them!' Tony sat back into the armchair, shaken by David's words.

'My God, David, this is terrible, what's going to happen? Can't we do something about it?'

David held up his hand. 'This is why I have asked you to come along this morning, Tony. You know how much I love Peter.'

'Of course I do,' agreed Tony, 'and I love him too. We have been friends forever. I would do anything for him, in spite of what's happened between us.'

'I'm glad to hear you say that, Tony, because now comes the time for me to ask you to put yourself in danger for Peter's sake.'

'OK. You tell me what you want me to do and I'll do it, David. I don't care what it is!'

David got out of his chair, walked over to the door, paused, and turned to face Tony.

'I want you to go to Birmingham, get Peter and the girl out safely, and hide them in a secure place until this has blown over. Can you do that, Tony?'

Tony was obviously excited about the prospect.

'Yes, I certainly can and will do it. And I'll get all the help I need. Leave it to me, David, I'll keep them safe!'

David felt relieved now that Tony had agreed to take on the project. He knew he would be able to devote more time to Rene's needs.

Feeling the inside of his coat pocket, he pulled out an envelope and handed it to Tony.

'Right, take this, there's five thousand pounds there for expenses. If you need any more, let me know. Money is no object where this is concerned. You'll find the address where they are staying inside the envelope.'

Tony took the money.

'OK David, don't worry about a thing. It will be sorted.'

'Oh! I'll let them know you are coming. As soon as you get organised, make sure you keep me informed.' David saw Tony get into a taxi and go off on his way.

Shirley came down the stairs as he entered the hallway.

'What was all that about, David?' she asked.

'I'm just being a bit old–fashioned, Shirley. I just wanted to be reassured of his intentions in the future regarding my grandchildren. I'd prefer it if he wasn't around them in the future.'

'Don't worry, I have made that clear to him, and he seems to have accepted the inevitable.' Shirley smiled.

'Come on then, David, we had better get cracking. Mum will be wondering where we are! We'll go in my car if you like. I've got to pick the kids up on the way back. Then I'm going to cook you a lovely dinner.'

'That sounds a great idea, Shirley,' replied David rubbing his hands together.

David and Shirley left Basildon Hospital at about six thirty in the afternoon. They were both very pleased with Rene's progress over the last couple of days. The consultant had told them that it was reasonable to keep stroke patients in for around a month, for tests and observation.

After leaving the leafy countryside of Paglesham by cab, Tony picked up his own car and proceeded to drive to his mother's home on the Dale Farm estate, near the town of Billericay, where he knew eviction for all the residents was imminent, including his own family. When he arrived, the place was busy as usual, with people gathered talking outside in the sunshine. Tony drove past several static caravans and permanent homes, after which he arrived at the familiar surroundings of his mother's dwelling. Getting out of the car, he waved to some friends as he made his way to the front door. Going inside, he was greeted by a short dark woman rather plump in stature and with a bright floral apron around her waist.

'Hello, Tony, where have you been?'

'Hello, Mum,' he replied, bending down to give her a kiss on the cheek.

'Oh, out and about,' she said dismissively.

'Do you know where Tom and Kevin are, Mum?' he asked.

'No, I haven't seen them since breakfast. They are probably still out on the lorry working.'

'Yeah,' he agreed.

'Why? What do you want your brothers for?' his mother queried.

'Nothing important, Mum,' he lied. 'I'll see them when they get back.'

Tony got the chance sooner than he expected. His brothers came speeding down the narrow lane in a battered old lorry and pulled up in a cloud of dust outside their mother's shack. They greeted him with a bear hug. They had always looked out for each other since they were old enough to appreciate the dangers that can be waiting round any corner. Tony explained to them the situation Peter had found himself in and told them everything about the job he had to do. He also told them they would each get one thousand pounds for helping him. Tom and Kevin Harman were twins, and were six years younger than Tony. Kevin had just been released from Wormwood Scrubs after spending eighteen months inside for GBH, while Tom was currently on probation, serving one hundred days' community service for stripping the copper from a church roof! They were both big lads, over six feet two and weighing in at sixteen stone apiece. Not to be taken lightly.

They both readily agreed to take on the job. They all knew where to go to get tooled up, which they needed to do, considering the opposition they were dealing with.

CHAPTER 16

MUTUAL GOALS

Tony, Kevin, and Tom set off for Birmingham at approximately half past two in the afternoon, planning to arrive at the hotel at around five to five thirty.

At exactly the same time, David rang Peter. Peter and Sophia were just in the middle of a late lunch when Peter picked up the phone.

'Hello, Dad,' he said smiling. 'Any news?'

'Hello, Son,' David replied. 'Yes, listen carefully, I've had to recruit someone else to come and get you and Sophia out of Birmingham, because I don't really want to leave Rene too long.'

'All right, Dad, that's OK as long as they can be trusted?'

David decided to put the ball in his son's court.

'Yes, David, I couldn't agree more. We don't want any slip–ups, do we?' David continued confidently.

'Peter, who would you choose if I asked you to pick out someone that you would trust with your life?'

'Mmmmm . . . well, Dad . . . if you had asked me that question eighteen months ago, I would have had no hesitation in saying Shirley and Tony! Why do you ask that?'

'Yes, I knew you would say that, putting aside for the time being the recent history between you, Shirley, and Tony and the consequences of that affair. Tony is still your friend, and he would do anything it takes to say he's sorry and rekindle your friendship. And before you say anything, they are not together any more.'

Peter sounded a bit shocked.

'Are you saying Tony is coming to pull us out of here, Dad?'

'Well . . . yes, I am. Tony is the best one I know off who would not be afraid if he ran into trouble. But not only that, he will look after you better than anyone else I know.'

'All right, Dad, you've convinced me. I know what you're saying is true . . . but I shall never forgive him for betraying me the way he did! What time is he leaving?'

'He said he would be leaving at roughly two thirty. That's just about now.'

'OK, Dad, I'll make sure everything's ready. Goodbye.'

Sophia was looking at David with a little smile playing on her lips. 'Did I get that right? The chap that seduced your wife is coming to rescue us?'

'Yes, you heard right, darling. I had to agree with Dad. Tony is the best person to be on your side in times of impending trouble. He should be here in about three hours. We had better pack so we are ready to go as soon as he arrives.'

Peter suddenly brought his hand up and covered his eyes.

'Oooh dear, my head.' Sophia immediately rushed over to where he was standing, placed her hands on his shoulders, and guided him to the bed. Peter, still holding his head, sat down.

'Oh, Sophia, the pain in my head is murder.'

Sophia got down on her knees and took hold of his hands.

'Where exactly is the pain, darling?'

Peter indicated the area the pain was coming from with his fingers.

'It's just about there.'

'Does it hurt when you press it?' she asked.

'No,' Peter replied.

'In fact, its going now,' said Peter, smiling.

Sophia wrapped her arms around him and pulled herself up on to the bed, pushing him over on to his back in the process. Nuzzling up to his ear, she whispered, 'Don't worry, darling, you are going to get some pain over the next two or three months. You are still in the recovery process.'

Peter moved his head so he could kiss her forehead.

'But how long does this go on for?' He sounded slightly agitated.

'That's a very good question, darling, and one that I can't answer, nor can anyone else for that matter.'

'Why not, for goodness sake?'

Sophia began to feel she was starting to give a lecture, but she felt Peter deserved some sort of explanation as to what could be expected in the coming months, leading to his, hopefully, full recovery. He was too intelligent to be treated with anything less.

'Peter, doctors have no reliable way to predict the outcome of seemingly minor head trauma. You won't know for certain whether your injury is mild or moderate until at least another four or five weeks have passed. If you feel pretty much back to normal in a couple of months, then the injury would be classified as mild.

'And with my experience dealing with many types of head injury, I would say, although you had a very nasty accident which required surgery to your skull, you did not suffer damage to the brain. Therefore, you won't need "Cognitive Rehabilitation". That's when your thinking becomes impaired, and you have to go through a re-learning process. So, darling, you were very lucky for it not to have been a lot worse! But you might have the odd headache, and you may go into dark moods now and again. If and when that happens, I'll be here to see you through them.'

Peter lay on the bed taking it all in and thinking how wonderful she was. They sat up together. Peter took her into his arms and kissed her on the mouth; she responded passionately.

CHAPTER 17

THOSE WHO DARE

Tony cursed the driver who had just cut him up. They were halfway to completing the journey to Birmingham; he looked at the clock; it read 1545 hrs. About on schedule, he thought to himself. Both Kevin and Tom were snoring. Kevin was laid out on the back seat, while Tom was crunched up in the front, with his knees up to his chin, both out for the count.

With nothing to do other than drive the Mitsubishi Shogun, Tony found his mind starting to wander back over the last eighteen months or so. He thought about Peter, one of the best friends a man could wish to have. What he had done to his friend was one of the worst psychological blows he could have delivered. Of course he fancied Shirley; she was a beautiful woman with a great personality. They had had lots of fun together while Peter was away working. But he knew, whenever he was in that role, he was within a circle of complete trust, looking after his friend's family. And he broke that trust. Yes, they were both drunk at the time, and he had tried to accept that as a valid reason for their actions. His conscience would not allow him to do that. And then when Peter moved away and more or less disappeared from the scene, he somehow found himself taking over his friend's position –husband and father—which he now realised was adding insult to injury. He knew it was all over between him and Shirley. And he couldn't help but feel sorry for her, more so after what David had told him about Peter meeting someone else. He knew that he had been a ready-made convenience as far as she was concerned. She had remained totally in love with Peter throughout. Now her mind was set on getting him back. Tony shook his head and made himself take more of an interest in the traffic ahead of him. His thoughts were making him very depressed.

Tom stirred as he started to come back to life.

'Are we there yet, Tony?' he yawned.

'We should be in Birmingham in about an hour,' replied Tony, without taking his eyes off the road.

'I think we'll go straight to the hotel and pick them up! A quick turnaround, so we can get back as soon as possible.'

That last remark of Tony's made Kevin rear his head from behind.

'Bloody hell, Tony, I'm starving, can't we stop and get a cuppa at least?'

Tony let rip at his whining brother, 'What the hell's the matter with you, Kevin? You've been asleep all the way, you're getting paid good money for doing this, and all you can think of is your guts! This is very important. I've already explained to you the sort of people we are dealing with. So the quicker we get it done, the better it will be for all concerned. Do you understand, Kevin, do you get my drift?'

Kevin didn't like his older brother shouting at him.

'Yes, OK . . . Tony . . . sorry!'

'All right, keep your mouth shut until I tell you to open it.'

Tony and his brothers were about half an hour away from the hotel.

Phil and Harry, provided they didn't get any hold–ups, would reach the hotel approximately ten minutes before them. After having discovered the information about where Peter's father was staying, they had immediately relayed the address to Brett, who told them to return and find out if she was there. Phil remembered his words, 'If you find them, let me know immediately, then take them to the Stratford factory and wait there for me.'

'You all right, darling?' the question came from Peter as he put his arm around Sophia.

'Yes, Peter, I'm OK, they'll be here in a minute, won't they?'

'Yes, in five minutes or so, have you got everything together?'

'Sophia, why are you shaking?'

'I don't know, Peter, I'm beginning to feel a bit scared,' she answered quietly. Peter wrapped his arms around her and held her close to him.

'There's nothing to be scared of, my darling. Tony and his brothers will look after us.'

'Yes, I'm sure they will. It's just that — well, it feels like I have found what I've always yearned for. To be able to trust someone completely, and to feel so relaxed with them can usually only be achieved over a long period of time. I have got it with you and I never want to lose it.'

"I promise you, Sophia, you will never, ever lose it. We have both found in each other a very rare bond . . . something you could search for all your life . . . and never find.

Phil drove into the hotel car park. Selecting a space, so they were not near to other cars, he turned to Harry. 'When we get into the room, leave the talking to me. If they're there, I want them to come quietly. We don't want to cause a scene, and some nosey old bastard calling the police!'

Harry agreed, and with that, they made their way in to the reception area. Phil told Harry to wait while he got the room number.

The young receptionist greeted him with, 'Can I help you, sir?'

Phil was very polite, 'Yes, I would like the room number of Mr Doddington please, miss.'

'And who shall I say is calling, sir?'

'Oh no . . . I don't want you to tell him I'm coming . . . it's a surprise!'

'I see, sir, it's Room 432,' she replied with a beautiful smile. Phil thanked her and rejoined Harry.

'You ready, Harry?' he asked as he walked towards the lifts. Harry jumped up from the armchair in the lounge area and followed Phil. They were the only occupants in the lift. Phil pressed the button that would take them to floor four. A mechanical female voice told them the doors were closing. The lift went to number four without stopping at two and three. Door's opening. Three seconds later, the doors opened. There was no one outside waiting. Phil and Harry proceeded along the carpeted hallway looking at the numbers: Twenty-two, twenty-four, twenty-six, twenty-eight, thirty. There it was: number thirty-two. Phil reached out and tapped on the door.

Peter and Sophia both jumped up together when they heard the knock on the door. They looked at each other for a couple of seconds before Peter held his hand up as a signal to Sophia to be silent.

'Who is it?' Peter asked in a calm voice.

Phil answered authoritatively, 'Mr Doddington?'

'Yes,' Peter confirmed.

'Oh hello, Mr Doddington, I have a letter to be delivered to you personally.'

'OK, can you slip it under the door, please?'

'Afraid I can't do that, sir, you have to sign for it!'

Peter looked at Shirley for guidance. Spreading her hands out, Shirley whispered, 'Go on, open it, sounds genuine enough!'

'OK, just a minute,' he said as he released the catch and opened the door. As soon as the door started to open, Harry put his shoulder to it and shoved unceremoniously. Peter was literally knocked off his feet, as Phil and Harry tumbled into the room. Phil shut the door behind them. Shirley ran to Peter's side as he lay dazed on the floor.

Phil spoke first, 'At last, it's been quite a journey, trying to locate you two. And I can tell you this for nothing. Brett is so not happy with you, Shirley!'

Peter, with a little help from Sophia, slowly got back on his feet and said, 'Look, what do you want? If it's money, I can get it . . . whatever it is.'

Phil laughed out loud.

'Money! Money! You must be joking, mate. The boss has more money than Barclay's Bank. No, I'm afraid he wants more than that from you. He wants your blood, sonny! You do not cross a man like Brett Carlodo. If you value your time on this planet, I can tell you!'

He continued, 'And as for you,' nodding his head in Sophia's direction, 'You must out of your tiny mind, because you know what he's capable of!'

Sophia turned and faced Phil.

'Phil, you know how he treats me, you've seen it with your own eyes. And yet you are doing this. If you need to take me, I'll go with you. But leave Peter alone. It's got nothing to do with him. It was me that started it!'

Peter stepped forward and placed himself in front of Sophia.

'You'll take her over my dead body, you bastard!' he said raising his fist at Phil.

'Well, I'll tell you what, Peter, or whatever your name is, that can very easily be arranged here and now. And I would have no feelings of guilt in doing it. But unfortunately, I would be committing suicide, simply because Brett needs to meet you in the flesh, alive and in good health, know what I mean? So if we did anything to damage you in any way, well, you get the picture, I'm sure!'

Phil's tone changed as he ordered, 'Right, that's enough chatter, get your things together and let's go.' And to emphasise his authority, he pulled out a handgun and waved it in the direction of the exit.

'If you think there will be any hesitation in me using this, if I'm forced to, then you are very much mistaken. So do yourselves a big favour, don't cause any trouble, all right?'

Peter sounded nervous.

'Where are you taking us?' he questioned.

'That's for me to know and you to find out,' he sneered.

'I know where you're taking us,' cut in Sophia.

'Please, Phil, let us go. We promise we won't say anything to anybody, will we, Peter!'

'Don't waste your breath, Sophia,' Peter replied.

'They've no intention of letting us go.'

Phil made Sophia put her arm through his, as they walked out of the lift and into the reception area. Harry kept Peter close to him by discreetly holding on to his arm. They continued in that position as they walked towards the car park.

Tony pulled into the hotel car park, found a space just across from the main entrance, killed the engine, and got out of the car, glad to stretch his legs. Kevin and Tom were about to follow suit, when Tony shouted in panic.

'Don't get out of the car, stay where you are.' Quickly jumping back in, he carried on, 'Duck down as low as you can.'

'What the hell's going on?' yelled Kevin, doing as he was told, getting as low down in the seat as he could. Tom was calmer. 'What's up, bruv?' he murmured. Tony couldn't believe what he had just seen.

'Peter and two other men have just come out of the hotel, and there's a girl with them.'

'Blimey,' uttered Kevin.

'That must be the ones who are after them.'

'Kevin, you should have been a rocket scientist,' joked Tom as he gingerly tried to peep over the top of his seat, until receiving a reprimand from his older brother.

'For Christ's sake, keep your bloody head down, Tom, they are walking past the car.' All three of them kept well down for a full two minutes. Tony told his brothers to stay down. As he slowly raised himself high enough to see over the top of the seat, he had timed it perfectly. He could see the four of them getting into a Land Rover.

Talking in a whisper, he gave a running commentary on the situation, 'They are just getting into the car now. It's now moving towards us.'

'Tony, why are you whispering?' asked Kevin.

'I can hardly hear what you're saying!' Tony suddenly felt like an idiot. He grinned at Kevin's words.

'I don't know, Kevin,' he said.

'I must be losing me marbles!' The Land Rover passed out on to the main highway. Tony started the engine and followed at a discreet distance.

'You can both sit up now,' he said. The Land Rover was about four vehicles ahead of them. Tony thought he would try and keep that distance consistent if he could.

Tom sounded surprised when he said, 'It looks as though they are heading for London.'

'Yes,' said Tony, 'it certainly looks that way.'

Kevin leant over the back seat questioning, 'What are we going to do, Tony?'

Tony shook his head.

'That, Kevin is a very good question,' he answered. 'And one I honestly haven't got the answer to yet!'

'We have got to think of something, Tony.' Tom sounded anxious.

'If we lose them, God knows what might happen.'

Tony didn't appreciate the continued interruption of his thoughts.

'All right, all right! I know we have to do something,' he shouted. 'And that's what I'm trying to do, wracking my brains for a solution.

What do you expect? Do you want me to fly out of the window like Superman and grab them out of the car?'

'Oh yeah, very funny,' mused Tom.

'Well, come up with some sensible suggestions then!' said Tony.

The inside of the vehicle went strangely silent for a full five minutes. It was Tony who spoke first.

'I can't think of any way we can plan this out,' he said, shaking his head.

'But what I do know is, to do nothing would be crazy.'

'So we have to grab the opportunity when it presents itself.' Kevin piped up. 'When will we know that, Tony?'

Tony, trying to be patient, answered, 'Don't worry about that, Kevin, I'll let you know!' He grinned at the smile playing around Tom's lips.

The M1 stretched in front of them; the Land Rover was doing a steady speed of sixty mph, and Tony had no difficulty in keeping up.

'What do you think the chances are of them catching on that they're being followed, Tony?' asked Tom.

'Tony scratched his head before he responded to the question. 'Well, put it like this, Tom, if that was me, in the same situation, I would be keeping a very sharp eye out for that sort of thing.'

'Yeah, but they're not all as clever as you, Tony, are they?' Kevin joined in.

'No, you're absolutely on the ball. I have got to agree with you there, Kevin,' said Tony laughing. And then, in a more serious note, 'But you can be too clever. It can turn out to be a fatal move, underestimating the opposition. I bet they are keeping watch!'

'But there's a lot of traffic going towards London, so I think they've got their work cut out nailing us, don't you?' Tom queried.

'Yes, Tom, I hope you're right,' answered Tony.

'I could do with a break, Tony,' said Kevin, 'I'm hungry!'

'Yeah, I know, Kev. We all could. If you want to go to the toilet, there's a big can in the back. You can go in that.'

'Yes, I know,' said Kevin, 'I've already been.'

'We are now about to join the M25. Something's got to happen soon, lads,' said Tony. Driving for another half an hour, the 4 x 4 they were following turned into the South Mimms services. Tony was holding his breath when he did the same.

Phil moaned to Harry as he was leaving the hotel car park, 'I didn't even have time for a piss.'

'We can stop at South Mimms and get a takeaway, can't we?' Harry asked Phil hopefully.

'Yeah, but we've got to be careful.'

'If you stop at South Mimms, can we go to the toilet, please?' Peter asked politely.

Phil laughed. 'No chance, mate, the only time you get out of here is the time you get to meet the guv'nor, and I can assure you, you won't like that much.'

Sophia cuddled up closer to Peter as she said, 'I'm so sorry for getting you into this mess, Peter. This is the very reason I didn't want to start any sort of relationship. I knew what would happen. Phil is right, I must be stupid! I don't care about myself. It's you I'm worried about.' 'What are we going to do?' Phil raised his voice. 'I thought I told you no talking. Any more of it and you'll get my hand across your face.'

Peter nudged Sophia and pointed at the South Mimms's sign that was presenting itself some distance ahead. She nodded and pulled herself even closer to him.

Phil checked his rear-view mirror before he pulled into the South Mimms services. He saw there were several cars doing the same thing. But he didn't notice anything untoward, it being what one would expect, leading to a service area. Phil selected a spot away from the other vehicles.

'Harry, I'm busting, keep the gun on them while I go to the toilet, won't be a minute.'

'No problem, Phil, I'll go when you get back.'

Having parked discreetly, behind another 4 x 4, Tony watched Phil leave the Land Rover. As soon as he was out of sight, he shouted to Kevin, 'This is the opportunity I was talking about, Kevin! Get behind the wheel, keep the engine running, and be ready to move when I say go-go-go.'

'Tom, come with me.'

As both of them ran towards the parked Land Rover, Tony gave hurried instructions to Tom.

Tony, having reached the driver's side, tapped on the window. Harry immediately looked over in that direction. In that second, Tom had opened the passenger door and brought his massive fist crashing into the left side of Harry's face; he flew backwards, crashed into the steering wheel, and didn't even twitch. Tony had already opened the rear door. Peter, with a look of amazement on his face, helped Sophia out, who looked completely dazed.

'Come on,' cried Tony, 'Run to the Shogun.' Peter, grabbing hold of Sophia's hand, sprinted across the tarmac and leapt into the back of the Shogun. 'Go! go! go!' Tony's voice rang out, and before he had time to shut the door, Kevin had put his foot down, making the big six cylinder motor roar as it cleared the car park, discarding a thin layer of rubber on the surface and joined the motorway, leaving a cloud of dust in its wake.

Phil came out of the toilet much lighter and more relaxed than when he went in. He was tempted to get himself a cup of coffee, when the aroma of fresh ground beans began to tickle his nostrils. But the image of Brett was a lot more powerful. So he was prompted to take the latter route.

His heart missed a couple of beats when, from a distance, he couldn't believe his eyes. The Land Rover's doors were wide open.

He broke into a jog; by the time he had reached the vehicle, he was seriously short of breath. But what he saw nearly finished him off!

Harry was lying wedged up against the wheel, his face covered in blood. Phil tried to lift him into a sitting position. Harry moaned as he started to regain consciousness. Phil had blind panic in his voice.

'Harry, what happened to you? Where have they gone?'

Harry moaned again.

'Ohooo,' he groaned, 'What happened?'

'That's what I would like to know!' shouted Phil.

Harry was sitting up holding the side of his face.

'I think my jaw has been broken, Phil, I'll have to get to the hospital.'

'What hospital is that then? Harry, do you know of a particular one around here? What are you going to say to them when they ask you how you did it, tripped over a kerb?'

'Don't be so bloody sarcastic, you bastard, this hurts when I talk.'

'Well, you better keep your mouth shut then, hadn't you? It's what Brett is going to say, or do, that worries me. He told me to take them to Stratford where he would meet us. When he finds out we had them in our grasp and then let them go, do you think he will give us a bonus?'

'Did you phone him and tell him that we were on our way then?' asked Harry with great difficulty, and obviously in pain.

'Wait a minute! Yes, you're right. I did try to ring him after we left the hotel, but I couldn't get a signal.' Utter relief was etched on Phil's face as he remembered cursing, because he couldn't tell Brett the good news.

'Right, Harry, this is what we're going to do. I'll phone Brett and tell him we couldn't find Sophia. He can't prove otherwise. We'll then go back home.'

Harry shook his head. 'That's all very well, Phil, but if he ever finds out that we double-crossed him, we'll both end up as sausage meat in one of his restaurants.'

'Yes, I know that, Harry, but he won't find out, will he? Neither of us is going to tell him and nobody else knows, do they?'

'Sophia and that Peter know,' whined Harry.

'So the boss will find out when he catches up with them. All right, Phil, I'll leave it up to you, I just want to go to sleep.'

Having made up his mind that it was the best way to safeguard their self–preservation, Phil phoned Brett. It was picked up.

'Yes,' came a curt answer.

'Oh, hello there, boss, it's Phil speaking, err . . . err, thought I'd better let you know we couldn't find them, err, I mean they wasn't at the hotel!'

His heart was doing overtime as he tried to justify the words he heard coming out of his mouth. He was finding it difficult to sound convincing, knowing he was talking to the one man he was petrified of. He knew above everything else that if Brett Carlodo ever found out he had been lying to him, he had just signed his own death warrant.

Brett didn't sound very pleased.

'Did you make enquiries at the reception desk?'

'Well . . . err, yes . . . they said they had left.' Phil could feel trickles of perspiration starting to run down his back.

Brett pressed on. 'Did you ask if they had left a forwarding address?'

'Err . . . err, well, err I didn't, no, I didn't think they would have given it to me, boss!'

Brett was angry. Phil could visualise his face getting redder.

'You stupid bastard, you didn't give them the chance to refuse. Get back in there and see if you can get any information as to where they've gone, are you still at the hotel?'

Phil was starting to lose it.

'Well, err, no boss, not exactly.'

'Then where in the hell are you exactly?'

Phil was trying to extract himself from a very dangerous conversation. He felt the longer it went on, the deeper the hole would become, ending with him being buried alive.

'Just getting some fuel, boss,' he ventured.

'All right, as soon as you've filled up, get back to the hotel. If I get time, I'll meet you there. If not, I'll expect you back at the house, is that clear enough for you?'

'Yes, boss, understood,' Phil spluttered and rang off.

Kevin kept the Shogun at a steady seventy miles an hour as they headed towards Basildon on the M25.

When Sophia and Peter had recovered enough to start talking, they couldn't stop!

It was as though nothing had happened between Peter and Tony to ruin the special relationship.

'Tony, I have never been so pleased to see anyone in my life, as when I realised it was you and the boys who were pulling us out of the car! I thought we were goners.'

'What?' screamed Sophia. 'You didn't say that to me when we were being kidnapped!'

'Well, no, darling, I didn't. Do you really think I would tell you what I was really thinking?'

Sophia shook her head wistfully, 'No, of course, you wouldn't. And to be honest, nor would I!'

'I don't know how we will ever find the words to thank the three of you,' said Sophia, looking at Tony, who was sitting next to Peter.

'Sophia, you don't have to thank us at all. This is what friends, real friends, do for one another. We look after each other!'

'Where are we going, Tony?' butted in Peter.

'Well, until we get something properly sorted, you're staying with us . . . at my mum's place, you know . . . in Billericay. No one will find you there.'

'Don't be too sure about that, Tony!' alerted Sophia.

'He won't give up that easily, more so now that you have beaten him once. He'll be all the more determined to get what he wants. That's revenge pure and simple.'

'Well, don't worry your pretty little head about that, Sophia,' Tony answered. 'If he comes anywhere near Dale Farm, him and his cronies will get more than they bargained for I can tell you.'

'I'll vouch for that, Sophia,' Peter promised. 'I'm glad Tony's people are on our side, because I sure as hell wouldn't like to be against them.'

'You don't know how relieved it makes me feel to hear you all talk so positive about it,' said Sophia. 'I'm actually beginning to believe I'm going to get out of this alive!'

'Well, you had better believe it,' piped up Kevin. 'Because nobody gets past the Harman boys! Am I right, lads!'

Tony and Tom both agreed with a loud y-e-e-e-s in unison. They all laughed out loud, enjoying the moment, letting the build-up of adrenaline gradually subside.

David switched his mobile off as he was going back into the hospital to rejoin Shirley and her mother. He had just been talking to Peter, who had completely updated him on the sequence of events since the last time they spoke. David was horrified to think that they both (Sophia and Peter) were kidnapped by that terrible man. He secretly thanked God that Tony was able to pull off a minor miracle, and would now get them to a place of comparative safety. For now at least, he was under no illusions that the trouble would stop. The man seemed to be too obsessive, and was an obvious schizophrenic. So he was very unlikely to give up at the first hurdle. David had been careful not to sound like a father talking to a young child, when he advised Peter to be very alert to anything suspicious and not to take any unnecessary chances. He also told him the reason he had left the hotel in such a hurry. David was very pleased for him.

When David re-entered the ward, Rene was sitting. Propped up by three white pillows, Shirley looked up and smiled as he moved towards them.

'Hello, David, everything OK?'

'Yes,' replied David, as he leant over and kissed Rene on the cheek, 'everything's just fine!' He sat down in the chair on the other side of the bed and took hold of Rene's hand.

'And how is my little chocolate drop?' he mused.

Rene was gradually getting to form words and making sounds.

'I'm-arrl-the-b-bete for-sherig-yuu,' she managed, giving David a smile. At that moment, they were interrupted by one of the nurses. 'The doctor would like to talk to one of you about Mrs Staples, please.' Shirley and David moved their chairs back at the same time. 'Oh, go on, Shirley, you go,' said David, starting to sit down again.

'No, you can go, David, you can tell me all about it later!'

David immediately jumped up from his chair. 'All right, darling, thank you,' he said as he disappeared out of the door.

The nurse ushered David into the consultant's room; the doctor stretched out his hand as David closed the door behind him. 'Have a seat, Mr Doddington.' David shook his hand. 'David, please,' he said as he sat down on the chair.

'Don't get worried or anything, David, this is just a routine chat, just to put you in the picture, and bring you up to date with your fiancée's condition and also to answer any questions you may have regarding her care.'

'Thank you, Doctor, there are one or two questions I would like the answers to.'

'All right, David, please go ahead and I will answer them to the best of my ability.'

'Well,' began David, 'an obvious question is, can you determine the extent of damage to her brain, if any?'

'I am afraid I cannot answer that,' answered the doctor. 'We are going to have to wait and see how she progresses over the next couple of months and also what the results of the tests are. It's very early days.'

'What I can tell you is she was admitted very quickly, and that can be a major factor in how a stroke progresses. The longer it's allowed to go untreated, the more likely there will be permanent damage.'

'I see,' said David, 'another thing I would like to know is how long will she have to be in here.'

'Well again, it depends a lot on the tests' results. You see, there are two basic forms of stroke therefore they affect the person in different ways.'

He paused. 'David, do you know much about the nature of strokes?'

'Well, I must admit, Doctor, I don't, but I am naturally a curious individual. I do like to know about the nitty-gritty of things. Of course, now that I am personally involved, I really need to get all the relevant information on the subject I can,' explained David.

'That's what I like to hear, David, a man after my own heart!' The doctor carried on, 'Well, first of all, when the blood supply to the brain is interrupted or blocked for any reason, the consequences are usually drastic. Control over movement, perception, speech, or other mental or bodily functions is impaired, and consciousness itself may be lost. Disruptions of blood circulation to the brain are known as stroke, a disorder that occurs in two basic forms, both of which are potentially life-threatening. About three quarters of all strokes are due to the blockage of the oxygen-rich blood flowing to the brain. They are known as clots or ischaemic strokes. They are triggered by either a thrombus, which is a stationary clot that forms in a blood vessel, or an embolus, a clot that travels through the bloodstream and becomes lodged in a vessel. This type of stroke is often preceded by brief transient ischaemic attacks, or as we know them, TIAs, which are episodes of inadequate blood flow that may produce symptoms such as sudden physical weakness, an inability to talk, double vision, and dizziness. A TIA usually lasts for fifteen minutes or less. But they are a warning and of course should be taken very seriously. With a TIA, circulation and the vital oxygen supply are quickly restored and lasting brain and nerve damage is avoided. But with any stroke, however, the interruption of blood flow lasts long enough to kill brain cells, producing irreversible damage.

'The second basic type of stroke is bleeding stroke, or cerebral haemorrhage. It occurs when a brain aneurysm ruptures or when a weakened or inflamed blood vessel in the brain starts to leak. An aneurysm is a pouch that balloons out from a weakened spot on the wall of an artery. As blood flows into the brain, the build-up of pressure may either kill the tissue directly or destroy cells by impeding normal circulation to the affected region. This usually produces an excruciating headache, sometimes followed by loss of consciousness.

'But having said all that, I think I can more or less guarantee her being a resident for another three to four weeks!'

David felt depressed after hearing what the doctor had said. But he was pleased he had at least been honest with him.

He stood up. 'Thank you, Doctor, for the information.'

'No problem. Anything else I can help you with, please let me know.'

David made his way slowly back to where Shirley was sitting with her mother. Before he entered, he stood by the doorway looking at them together. They couldn't see him; he noticed Rene had lain down and appeared to have fallen asleep. Shirley was lovingly holding her hand and very quietly crying. He was forced to turn away and walk a little way down the corridor in order to regain his composure, before returning to the ward.

CHAPTER 18

FALSE INNOCENCE

Brett had been up since 6 a.m. He was in no mood to tolerate incompetence from anyone. His breakfast that morning consisted of three slices of thick fatty bacon, three new-laid eggs, fresh tomatoes, two pork sausages, button mushrooms, bubble and squeak, a slice of fried bread, two slices of toast and marmalade, washed down with two cups of sweet tea. He spread his morning newspaper over the garden table and placed his mug of tea down on top of it to stop the gentle breeze from blowing it across the lawn. He glanced at his watch: 0830 hrs. Sitting back in his chair, he let his eyes take in the beauty of his garden. It was a profusion of colour! There was no plan to the layout; you could say that it somewhat reflected the character of its owner. It was deviant in its order, with flowers growing adjacent to weeds, traces of green moss creeping out from under random stones. Grass needed cutting in various places, inviting a host of tiny insects to forage.

But, despite what some people might describe as a neglected garden, Brett loved its wild state and its natural charm, where nature was given a little bit of space . . . but Brett was still the boss!

Picking up his mobile, he called Phil. His patience was stretched to breaking point when it was not answered promptly. After three rings, he gave up and impatiently sent the phone spinning across the surface of the table, cursing under his breath.

'Snouty!' he yelled. Snouty came running into the garden as though trying to break the one-hundred-metre sprint record.

'Yes, boss.'

'Snouty, get hold of Phil and Harry, will you? And when you do, tell them I'm not very pleased with their efforts over the last twenty-four hours. I want to see them as soon as possible.'

'All right, boss, will do.' Snouty nearly bowed as he went back into the house.

Brett Carlodo was not used to being out of control in any situation. So to have a slip of a girl and her bloke making him look like an amateur was alien to him. The only way he knew of which could resolve the problem was to eradicate the source. As far as Brett was concerned, they had presented him with two options: one, take them both out (he knew of the right people who would manage that for him); and two, come up with a plan that would guarantee them coming into the open and presenting themselves to him with no fuss. In his twisted mind, he was very sure of the outcome on both counts. Exactly the same! He would come out on top. The fact that, in pursuing that dangerous path, he was also putting his whole operation in jeopardy didn't even enter his warped mind! The make-up of his schizophrenic nature meant he possessed the very dubious ability of being able to set aside all other aspects of his life and only focus on achieving total inner satisfaction. It was another two and a half hours before Snouty announced that he had managed to get hold of Phil and Harry. They were on their way to see him as requested.

Harry led the way sheepishly into the library where Brett was then spread out in one of the big armchairs. Phil was following behind as though trying to hide in Harry's shadow.

'Close the door behind you and sit down.' Brett's voice came across surprisingly calm, which worried Phil.

'Good morning, boss!' he ventured.

Brett didn't answer; he just sat there staring at them with his hands in his lap. It stayed like that for a full thirty seconds. Both of them were getting obviously fidgety, looking around the room at nothing and then at each other but never at Brett.

At last, he spoke, 'So you think it's a good morning, do you, Phil? And tell me the reason why you think it's a good morning.'

Phil turned his head and nervously stared at Harry, desperately seeking some sort of support.

Brett spoke again, 'Look at me, Phil, not Harry, he won't help you. Tell me, Phil, what part of the question did you not understand? I repeat, why do you think it is a good morning?'

Phil sat frozen in the chair; he was petrified that Brett had somehow found out about the episode of the day before.

'Well,' Phil found his voice, 'that's what people say when they meet each other in the morning, boss.'

'Oh, I see!' said Brett. 'So you're only saying it because other people say it,' sneered Brett. 'You don't really mean it then? Tell me, Phil, what other things do you say that you don't really mean, eh? Come on, Phil, speak up!'

'Nothing, boss, I don't say nothing I don't mean!'

'And what about you, Harry? Do you say things you don't really mean?'

Harry was somewhat taken by surprise by Brett's switch. 'Err, err, no, not me, boss,' he spluttered.

'You see, I'm not very happy with the way things turned out yesterday. I don't like the vibes I'm getting . . . you know what I mean. Is there anything you want to tell me while you have the chance, boys?'

Phil stuck to his guns, although he was scared; he had been working for Brett for too many years not to have learnt how to read him . . . up to a point!

'No, boss, we've told you everything that happened.'

Brett nodded his head. 'OK,' he said, 'that's all right then!'

Suddenly he smiled; his little game was over. 'Harry, what's the matter with your face?'

Harry immediately put his hand up and touched his injured jaw. 'I got into a fight, boss, down at the local. You should see the other bloke.'

Brett held up his hands. 'All right, enough of this, back to the business in hand. I want you both to go down to where Peter Doddington used to live, in Paglesham Essex. His wife still lives there, as you know. I want you to follow her every move, including who she meets, who she talks to, where she goes, and who she sleeps with! In fact, I want to know everything it is possible to know about somebody. Do I make myself absolutely clear?'

Phil and Harry answered in unison, 'Yes, boss.'

'And don't forget . . . keep me informed!'

Phil and Harry scuttled out of the room as though their very lives depended on it. When they emerged into the fresh open air, they felt as though they had just been reborn. They both knew that they had just slipped through Brett Carlodo's net.

CHAPTER 19

SAFE HOUSE

The Shogun was heading towards the Basildon turn-off where Kevin would leave the A127 and join the road to Billericay where his home was situated.

Peter sounded jubilant. 'Sophia, my darling, we are nearly home and dry! Thanks to these fellas.'

Sophia was laughing. 'I can't believe what you've done, Tony, it's like something out of a movie.'

Tony rubbed his fingernails up and down against his chest, at the same time raising his eyebrows, as he said, 'Oh, it's nothing, it's what we do!' he answered, joining in the laughter.

'Yes,' observed Peter. 'Tony always was a big-headed bugger.'

Sophia joined in, 'Well, I for one am pleased Tony is like he is, because if he hadn't been, we probably would not have got away today!'

Kevin was stuck at traffic lights at the beginning of Billericay High Street. Even after they had turned green, it didn't make a lot of difference to the movement of the traffic. Cars and vans were parked in the narrow road, causing havoc with the flow.

Kevin was getting impatient.

'Where's all the bloody traffic wardens? There's always plenty around when I'm parked where I shouldn't be!'

Tony ignored Kevin's remark and changed the subject by saying, 'Anyway, Sophia, it's not us you should be thanking, it's Peter's old man, because it was him that put this plan together and financed it.'

'Yes, I know, Tony, and don't you worry, I will thank him and let him know how grateful I am when I see him.'

'Which shouldn't be too long, Sophia. I think he's coming down soon,' Peter answered.

'It seems unusually quiet,' said Tom, as they drove on to the Dale Farm site.

'Well, it's nearly midnight, and if everyone is as tired as me,' exclaimed Sophia, 'I should think they are all in bed.'

Kevin pulled up outside his mum's house. Their mother came out before they had left their seats.

'About time, you boys, I was getting a bit worried, where have you been?' And then, she continued, 'Hello, who have we got here?'

Peter stepped forward, holding Sophia's arm. 'This, Margie, is Sophia, the love of my life, and this, Sophia, is the mother of these three scallywags and the best cook in the world.'

'Oh, Peter still knows how to turn the charm on, I see! Nice to meet you, Sophia, come on in to the house, darling, it's cold out here.'

They all trooped into Margie's dwelling, which Sophia thought was like the Tardis in Doctor Who, and said as much to Peter. Tom overheard the remark.

'Yes, you're right, Sophia, that's what happens when bits keep being added through the years! The front stays the same, but the back keeps growing.'

'Right,' said Margie, suddenly becoming all businesslike. 'I expect you're all hungry,' she shouted above the din. Everyone responded positively to her cry. 'Well, all go and sit down 'cause I've got a lovely pot of stew on the hob!'

After a really tasty and beautifully cooked meal, they were all ready for their beds. Tom and Kevin, who lived further down the road in their own place, said their good nights and left. Tony told them that he would see them in the morning and sloped off to his room. Margie led Sophia and Peter out to the back room.

'Here you are, you two. This is your room as long as you're here. You'll find it quite comfortable. It's a nice, soft double bed, so you should be all right.' She giggled as she said good night.

The sun shining directly on to Sophia's eyes woke her up. Stretching out her arm to find Peter, she grabbed at empty space. Pushing herself up into a sitting position, she was surprised to notice that the time was 10.15 a.m. Just as she was about to jump out of bed, Peter walked into the room.

'Good morning, darling.' He beamed. 'You slept well.'

'Hellooo, you,' she said, holding her arms out, letting the duvet fall away to reveal that she was completely naked. Peter came over and sat down beside her and took her in his arms. Their lips met in a soft, gentle brush. Then her tongue wriggled its way in between his teeth. She started to undo his belt. Without saying a word, Peter stood up and quickly took off his clothes and slipped under the cover. Sophia lay back as he gently kissed his way down, and there, he brought her to the peak of ecstasy. They finally got out of bed at 12.30 p.m. Then they were under the shower followed by lunch. Apart from them, there was no one else in the house. Peter said he had been up at about 0800 hrs and hadn't seen anybody.

'Is that usual, Peter?' she asked.

Peter was looking out of the window when he replied, 'Well, yes . . . it is really . . . I suppose.'

Sophia thought he seemed a bit preoccupied. 'What are you looking at, Peter?' she queried.

'I don't quite know, Sophia, there's something going on outside. There's a group of blokes talking and waving their arms about. It looks as though they are arguing over something.'

Sophia's curiosity got the better of her as she jumped up from the chair and joined him at the window. There were indeed five men huddled together keeping their voices low, so they could not hear what was being said.

Peter nuzzled Sophia's ear as he turned his head and whispered, 'What do you think that's all about then?'

Sophia looked a bit worried as she answered, 'They wouldn't be talking about us, would they?'

Peter looked a little surprised. 'Why would they be talking about us, for goodness' sake?'

'Oh, I don't know, Peter, I'm so wound up I've become suspicious of everything!'

'Yes, my darling, and I can understand that, but you must not allow yourself to become paranoid over it.'

It was another two hours before Tony came breezing through the door. 'Hello, you two, I've just popped in to talk about the rules that you both will have to abide by while you're here.'

'Good morning, Tony,' greeted Peter.

'Hello, Tony,' said Sophia, looking a bit puzzled. 'Rules? What rules?'

'Well, it's like this. The word has got out that, rightly or wrongly, the people round here think it is going to attract curiosity, and therefore trouble, because of the nature of your problem. Don't worry, they are not going to throw you off the site or anything like that . . . . It's just . . . well, they are a very superstitious lot. And, of course, everyone here is on tenterhooks at the moment because of the pending eviction notice! So they tend not to trust anybody.'

'So that was what they were talking about outside this morning!' exclaimed Peter, turning to look at Sophia.

'Yes, there you are, Peter, I said they could be talking about us, and you said I was getting paranoid!'

Peter leant across and gave Sophia a peck on the cheek. 'I apologise, darling, in future I shall listen to you!'

Tony sat down and explained, 'I have been talking to your dad this morning, Peter. He agrees with me that we have to treat this operation like a well-oiled machine. Just because we have tucked you away out of sight, you cannot afford to be complacent!'

Peter cut in, 'Tony, believe me, we both realise how lucky we are. And Sophia, more than anyone, knows what and who we are dealing with!'

Sophia chimed in, 'Yes, and also Tony, I know he is a very clever man. He has a host of influential professionals in his dirty hands. And believe me, Tony, they do his bidding because of the things he's got over them. When he say's jump, they obediently ask him how high!'

'OK, that's good,' replied Tony, 'you have both got the right attitude. Now while you're here, you must not set foot outside these premises, do you understand? And another thing, I don't want you looking out of the window at all. Now we have no way of knowing how long this is going to last, so I'm afraid you guys are going to have to be patient.' Tony laughed. 'I hope you don't end up getting on each other's nerves and doing a runner!' Sophia and Peter both joined Tony in the laughter.

'I really don't think there's much chance of that happening, my son, do you, Sophia?'

Sophia gave a big smile as she said, 'No chance, darling.'

'OK, as long as you both appreciate how crucial it is to be vigilant all the time, we stand a good chance of beating this,' said Tony. 'Now how about breaking open a bottle to celebrate?!'

'That's the best thing you've said today.' Peter grinned. 'Let's go for it.'

CHAPTER 20

SEEK AND YE SHALL FIND!

Both Phil and Harry made sure they had a good night's sleep before setting off once again for the Essex countryside. To ask if they were working under great stress would be like asking if Brett was going to give them a pat on the back when he eventually found out about the fiasco with Peter and Sophia!

It was playing on Phil's mind. He knew that if he didn't come up with the goods, Brett would take it out on him and Harry. He found himself asking, 'Is it worth it?' Although he had been working with Brett for a long time, he had noticed a significant change in his behaviour over the last six months or so. Brett had always been a ruthless individual, stopping at nothing to achieve the results that were right for him, not giving a damn how it affected other people, whether it was physical or monetary loss. He had not mentioned it to anyone, but he was terrified that, at any time, for the slightest reason, Brett could explode into bloody violence. He for one didn't want to be around when that happened.

Their orders were clear and specific. They were to keep as close to Shirley Doddington and her two children as the yolks in a double-yolked egg!

Harry put more pressure on the accelerator; the road was becoming less like a full car park.

'That's better,' observed Phil, when the speed picked up to hover around eighty miles an hour. They were about five miles from the village of Paglesham.

'What we going to do when we get there, Phil?' asked Harry.

Phil wearily shook his head. 'That is a very good question, Harry, I think we will have to play it by ear, mate. I'll tell you one thing, Harry, we have got to come up with the goods this time. I am not going to face Brett and tell him that we've failed again.'

Harry took his eyes off the road for a couple of seconds and looked across at Phil. 'Well, I can't see any alternative. If we don't get the information he needs this time, we'll just have to try something else.'

'Yes, Harry, you're right. That is the logical approach how we would go about it. And to be honest with you, that's what Brett would have done a few years ago.

'You know damn well Brett would never have bothered to chase down a bloody girl with so much vengeance. We've not been doing our usual jobs since all this happened! So look how much money he is letting go. I'll tell you, Harry, the big boys in London are not going to stand that for too long. You know that, as well as I do!'

'Well, then, we'll just have to make sure we do the business, Phil, won't we?' replied Harry.

They had reached their destination. There were no street lights; there were a few lights coming from a scattering of dwellings. But other than that, it was quite dark. Shirley's house was just visible from where they had parked. 'Get the bag of food and drink from the back, Harry, will you? I think we'll be here for quite some time!' By the time they satisfied their hunger with ham sandwiches and washed it down with coffee, it was past midnight. Harry curled up in the back of the Land Rover, while Phil settled himself in the front. They were jolted awake at 7.30 a.m. by the sound of heavy machinery, which turned out to be a rather large boat being towed towards the river. Phil sat up and noticed there was movement around the Doddington household. Shirley was putting the milk bottles out on the doorstep.

'Harry, make sure you're awake. It looks as though we'll be leaving any time now. That must be the wife that Brett wants us to follow.' Harry joined Phil in the front without a word. He fished around and found the coffee flask and proceeded to pour two cups. It was another hour before Shirley came out of the house, with Jamie and Josie in tow. Phil was behind the wheel of the Land Rover, as they kept a discreet distance from the car in front. Shirley dropped her son off at his school in Westcliff-on-Sea, then carried on to Billericay, where she pulled up at a large house just the other side of the town. Phil stopped a few hundred yards behind.

'I wonder who lives there,' said Harry.

'I don't know yet,' replied Phil, 'but I intend to find out pronto!' They watched as Shirley and her daughter disappeared into the house.

'What are we going to do now, Phil?' queried Harry.

'I'm just going to ring Brett, to let him know what's happening,' answered Phil.

Brett picked up his mobile. 'Hello, Phil.' He sounded in a good mood for change. It allowed Phil to relax somewhat. 'What you going to tell me?'

Phil gave Brett a complete rundown on the progress so far. Brett was satisfied up to a point. He stressed he wanted to know whose house the woman had gone into. (The woman he guessed was Mrs Doddington.) He wanted to know in the next hour. Phil promised he would get the information. Then Brett closed down.

'Hello, Shirley.' David kissed her on the cheek as she came through the door.

'Grandad!' called out Josie. David bent down, picked her up, and held her in his arms as he walked into the back of the house. Shirley closed the front door and followed them.

'Some good news from the doctor at the hospital last night, Shirley,' said David. 'I didn't ring you. It was getting a bit late by the time I got home.'

'Oh, what was that then?' asked Shirley.

'He said that he expected your mother to make a full recovery, but it is going to be a slow process.'

'That's fantastic news, David. It doesn't matter how long it takes as long as she gets better. We're going up to see her today, aren't we?'

David answered with excitement in his voice, 'Yes, and what's more . . . wait for it . . . she's coming home next week!'

Shirley couldn't believe what she had just heard. 'David, that's fantastic. If you had rung me last night, I wouldn't have slept a wink.'

'Right,' said David, ushering Shirley into a chair. 'You sit yourself down there while I go and make a cup of tea.' As he went into the kitchen, Josie trotted after him.

'How's Peter, David? Is he out of hospital yet?' Shirley tried to sound casual, but she caught David off guard with the sudden question.

'Err . . . well, yes . . . he is. He's actually gone down to Devon for a while. He's staying at a convalescent home for a couple of months.' He felt guilty having to lie to Shirley, but justified it by thinking that knowing the truth would hurt her even more.

'Oh, that's nice for him. Who arranged that then?'

'Well, actually I did,' lied David.

'Why didn't you tell me?'

'I didn't think you would be particularly interested.' David wanted the conversation to end.

'I'm not really, just curious,' Shirley replied, telling a lie herself.

Phil came out of the library at the top of Billericay High Street and got in the Land Rover beside Harry with a pleased look on his face.

'Good news?' asked Harry.

'Yes.' Phil grinned. 'I've found out who he is.'

Harry sat there looking at Phil. 'Well . . . are you going to tell me or not?'

'Yes, his name is David Doddington, and he is Sophia's boyfriend's father.'

Harry had a smile on his face at the news. 'We are doing quite well, Phil, don't you think?'

'Yes, I'm going to let Brett know right away.'

Brett, satisfied with the progress Phil and Harry were making, gave orders then to follow David instead of Shirley, and to keep him updated.

David and Shirley were sitting by Rene's bed. Rene was all smiles, admiring the beautiful bouquet of flowers that David had just presented her with.

She sounded excited. 'I'm coming home next week, Shirley.'

'Yes, I know, Mum, it's wonderful news, and you have got to take it easy when you get there.'

'I will have no choice, darling, not with David in charge. I've got to start minding my Ps and Qs!'

'Don't worry, Shirley. I'm going to make sure she doesn't get up to any mischief.'

Shirley made her feelings known as she expressed the way she felt about David and her mother. 'I am so pleased for the both of you. To watch you two together makes me a little envious.' She laughed. 'Whatever you're both on, I want some!'

Rene grabbed hold of Shirley's hand. 'Thank you, sweetheart, things will turn out OK, you'll see.'

Phil took a couple of pills from the small bottle, swigged them down with a gulp of bottled water, and lay back down on his seat. He'd sent Harry up to get something to eat at the hospital restaurant.

That was an hour ago. He was now very hungry and wanted to go to the loo. He was getting slightly agitated. It was another half an hour before Harry showed his face.

'Where the bloody hell have you been, Harry?' he shouted. 'I've been waiting here slowly starving to death.'

'Sorry, Phil, there was a massive queue.'

'All right, I'm going now. Any developments let me know.'

Harry nodded and settled down with the radio.

David and Shirley left Rene's bedside at 9.30 p.m. They drove back to David's house, where Shirley left with Josie in her own car. Phil let her go. At around 11 p.m., Phil watched as David left his house and proceeded towards Ramsdon Heath, a small village near Billericay. He pulled into Oak Road, with Phil not far behind. After a few hundred yards, the car in front suddenly came to a halt. The rear lights were switched off. Phil switched off the engine and doused his own lights. How quiet it was, he thought.

David had decided to go and talk to Peter about the conversation he'd had with Shirley about his fictional convalescing down in Devon! He lived only two miles from the Dale Farm. He arrived just after eleven. Margie answered the door and welcomed him into her house.

Phil and Harry watched as David went through the door and saw Peter, as clearly as if he had been standing in front of them, through the window. Phil immediately started the engine and reversed out the way he had come in, with a big smile on his face.

Back on the main road, Phil was ecstatic. 'Yes! Yes!' he shouted at the top of his voice. 'We did it, Harry. We did the business!'

Harry was laughing. 'Does this mean we won't be decapitated, Phil?'

'Well, I wouldn't be surprised if Brett didn't bung us a few quid.' Phil laughed. 'We can't let him know until tomorrow morning anyway, so I think we should try and get a bed for the night. I for one could do with a good night's kip.'

'Yeah, I couldn't agree more,' said Harry.

CHAPTER 21

REPELLING BORDERS

When David stepped inside Margie's house, he thought for one moment he'd just gone through the doors of his local pub! The smell of beer was overpowering. Not that he'd got anything against it. He was just a bit surprised to find them in the middle of a party, and he hadn't been invited! He was greeted by all of them . . . overenthusiastically! Tony, Peter, Tom, Sophia, Margie, and Kevin—he could see they were all slightly under the influence. Because he was stone-cold sober, it sent the alarm bells ringing—very loudly. He didn't want to spoil their fun, but he knew he was going to have to say something to make them all realise they were acting irresponsibly. Peter gave his dad a hug.

'Hello, Dad, what are you doing here at this time of night?'

'Hello, Son,' said David, 'I thought I'd better drop in to let you know that Rene is coming home next week, so I won't be living at home.'

They all gathered around David listening to what he was saying. 'What about you and Sophia? How are you coping?'

Sophia answered for Peter, 'Yes, David, we are having a great time.' She slurred.

'I'm sorry,' said David, 'but I want you all to gather around and listen to what I have to say.' They looked at each other, wondering what to expect. Someone turned off the television as David started to speak.

'Now, everyone, here is an important part in the ongoing situation involving Peter and Sophia. And you are all aware of the consequences, if it all goes wrong. It is quite literally a matter of life and death for both of them! Do you all agree with that statement?' As one, they gave the thumbs-up to that.

David continued, 'Then now we've established that, perhaps someone would kindly explain to me why on earth you are putting the whole plan in jeopardy by drinking and not being vigilant? I shouldn't have been able to get close enough to the door for me to knock on it. If I had been a bunch of Brett's gang, none of you would have stood a prayer.' He looked at Sophia. 'Am I right, Sophia?'

Sophia lowered her eyes as she answered nervously, 'Yes, you're absolutely right, David,' she said with conviction. 'I'm so sorry, David . . . '

'No, hang on, Sophia, you're not to blame,' Peter interrupted. 'If anyone is at fault, it's me.'

'Oh no, it's not your fault, Peter,' intervened Tony. 'I'm in charge of this operation. I've fallen down on the job. I have let you all down. David's right, it's my responsibility.'

David sat listening and marvelled at how quick they had all appeared to have sobered up!

'Right,' he said, 'as you are all willing to take on a share of the blame, it seems to me you have all learnt something from your mistake. And that is the most important aspect of this, not to apportion blame, but to make sure nothing like this ever happens again. I only hope that it's not too late!'

'Thanks, Dad,' said Peter, 'we have all been very stupid.'

'OK, Son, I'll see you in a couple of days.' David said his goodbyes and left.

Phil looked at his watch: 9.30 a.m.

'OK, Harry, I think it's time to call the boss, he should be up by now.'

They were sitting in the Land Rover on Oak Road, off Cray's Hill, after spending the night at a local B & B.

'Yeah, I agree, Phil, he should be up by now.' Phil dialled the number. Brett answered.

'Yes?'

'Hello, boss, it's Phil.'

'Yes, I know that, what do you want?'

Phil was nervous; Brett didn't sound in a very good mood. 'Err, err . . . I have got some good news, boss!'

Brett shouted down the phone, 'Well, get on with it, you idiot, what is it?'

'We have found them, boss, we know where they are!'

'If that is true, Phil, I shall be very pleased with you and Harry, very pleased indeed. Where are they?'

Phil went on and gave Brett the address.

'Now, Phil, listen to what I am going to say to you, it's very important. I am sending down four of the lads to help you bring them back. You are in complete charge, OK? I shall be holding you responsible for any mistakes.'

Phil didn't like that set-up at all. 'Boss, couldn't you put someone else in charge?'

'Phil, what you've got to do is stop bloody whingeing, and do as you're told. Now, don't spoil my day, get on with it.' The phone went dead.

The travellers who resided on the Dale Farm site were, to put it mildly, a very close-knit community. And therefore, any interference from outside sources, be it intentional or unintentional, was not received with any enthusiasm. Even the police were reluctant to enter the site for anything other than dire emergencies at the moment because of the sensitive nature of the eviction order hanging over the whole site like a big black cloud. So it came as no surprise to Tony when he was approached the night after the drinking session by one of the senior men and asked what was going on, and furthermore why had the 'council' not been informed? Tony held his hands up and admitted he should have put them in the picture. The man, whose name was Roger Davis, told Tony to be at an arranged meeting that night to discuss it with the council. And everyone involved was to attend.

Tony informed everyone when, where, and at what time the meeting would take place and the importance of a full attendance. The meeting was held at Roger's house. There were twenty members of the site council, and the meeting started at 8 p.m.

The meeting was chaired by Roger. Tony explained to the council the exact situation, with accounts given by Sophia, Peter, and David.

The council openly discussed the pros and cons. After much deliberation, they came to the decision that because of Tony's close ties with Peter, they would protect Sophia and Peter and therefore put a plan into place to ensure their future safety. They were five minutes away from closing the meeting, when a latecomer entered the room and apologised to Roger. They stood talking for a few minutes, after which, Roger again addressed the meeting. Everyone was talking at once.

'Can I have everyone's attention, please? George here has just told me something that I think everyone should know. He says that last night he came in very late, and he followed a Land Rover on to the site. He pulled off on to his drive and noticed the Land Rover had stopped. After a couple of minutes, it reversed back out and disappeared. George reckons they were watching Margie's house. Now, if he's right, the people you're trying to avoid know you are here!'

'Oh my God!' Sophia let out a gasp. 'Peter, what are we going to do now?'

'Don't worry, my dear,' said Roger, 'we are going to set up a security plan. They will get more than they bargained for if they come on site!'

Roger gathered the men together and formed a rota list. There was to be a twenty-four-hour lookout; also sufficient men were to be made available to repel any attempt on a snatch.

Phil and Harry waited patiently; they were sitting at the bar in the White Horse Pub in Billericay. Brett's people were due to arrive in about half an hour. Then they would proceed to Dale Farm.

Phil lifted his pint glass up to his lips and held it there while he spoke, 'Come on then, Harry, let's get this over and done with.'

He downed the last dregs of bitter. 'I told them to meet us at the corner of Oak Road.'

Two nights after the site meeting, Kevin was the duty lookout. It was a very dark night, no moon; low, thick, rain-filled clouds covered the sky.

Kevin was positioned about one hundred yards up the lane, sitting in his Shogun and backed into the trees, completely hidden from the road.

There was no mistaking the sound. Kevin recognised the low rumble of a diesel engine. As it drew nearer, he caught the flash of headlights which were suddenly extinguished along with the sound of the engine. Kevin immediately felt alarm bells and phoned through to Roger. The plan was activated, which meant fifteen of the biggest men from the site stood ready, motivated to have a good punch-up with anyone who tried to invade their territory.

From his hiding place, Kevin watched as six shadowy figures moved across his vision, heading towards the illegal dwellings. The six gang members walked down the lane, three on each side; each was armed with a handgun or a sawn-off shotgun. All that could be heard was the twittering of a few birds and the distant bark of a dog. At regular intervals, two men were hiding on either side of the road leading to the site, also armed with guns! Seven others were positioned in strategic places around the buildings, all of them armed. Phil had earlier told his army that he would lead them to the house, and three of them would stay back away from the scene ready to take care of any unforeseen happenings.

Phil went ahead and soon was in sight of the house; he indicated with a wave of his arm to let his mates know the location. Harry and a man named Mick joined Phil. They were being carefully watched by seven pairs of eyes. If they had thought to have looked above them and, of course, if it had not been so dark, they would have seen something they would not have liked. Hanging above them, stretched out across from one building to another, was a heavy wire net, ready to drop with a flick of a thin rope. Tony held on to the rope, waiting for a signal from Roger. The three gangsters approached the front of the house; Phil, gun in hand, made a move towards the door.

Roger raised his hand and made a thumbs-up sign to Tony, who gently jerked the rope. The heavy net fell straight and true, completely encapsulating the three rouges. The weight of the metal falling down from that height knocked the breath from their lungs and laid them flat on their backs. Tony and Roger ran forward and quickly lifted the net and retrieved the guns, as the men started to stir.

A voice came from the blackness. 'Stand still and put down those guns.' It came from one of the men who were told to hang back. Tony and Roger both looked up, got to their feet, and stood smiling at each other.

One of the men shouted, 'This is not a game, mate, this is a real gun, and it shoots real bullets.'

The three men were all standing together then; a voice right behind them said, 'Funny enough, so do these!' They were surprised to see another three people standing behind them, all with guns pointing. They then became completely surrounded by the rest of Roger's men coming out of the woodwork. By that time, Phil, Harry, and Mick had been hauled from underneath the net, looking extremely worst for wear. Roger's men had come ready for a fight, and they were not going to be denied.

One of the men shouted, 'Come on, lads, let's give the bastards a pasting.' The rest didn't need any encouragement; they waded in swinging their fists, kicking and punching, not getting it all their own way. In the end, Brett's gang gave up the ghost and ran for their cars, leaving the guns and their dignity behind.

CHAPTER 22

EXTREME MEASURES

Sir Richard Palestine was a much-respected gentleman by all who knew him. He was the chairman of several very successful national and international companies. He was a multi-billionaire. In addition, to being an advisor to the government of the day, he also, along with a couple of dozen other people who were in the same category, indirectly controlled the lives of every individual who chose to live in the United Kingdom. That did not exclude the criminal fraternity. That influential team met every six months to decide how much revenue to invest, where it was to be invested, which stock to sell, and which to buy, therefore influencing the financial markets, guiding the way they wanted for the next six months.

The team were sitting round a massive solid oak table, on the top floor of an office tower, somewhere in the city of Westminster. They had nearly concluded their business. There was just a small matter that gave cause for concern about one of the people who the syndicate used now and again, when it suited them. It had been brought to the attention of the team that that person was not conducting himself in a proper and businesslike manner and therefore was likely to draw adverse attention to himself and to other people in his private and business life. The verdict of the team was that he should cease to do

business immediately. Brett Carlodo had at last met his match . . .
but he didn't know it yet.

Phil, Harry, and the rest of Brett's boys jumped into their vehicles
and drove like maniacs away from the travellers' site and headed
back towards London, all battered and bruised, with their tails as
far between their legs as they could get them.

Sophia was still visibly shaken. Two hours had passed since the
siege had taken place. They had not achieved their objective, but
it had left Sophia and Peter very fearful of their lives. Tucked away
as they had been for the last few weeks, it had lulled them slightly
into a false sense of security. Roger of the council, Peter, Sophia,
Tony, David, Tom, and Kevin gathered together in Margie's house.
They all agreed on one thing: Peter and Sophia had spent their last
night at Dale Farm! That now presented another problem: where
were they to go now?!

Peter didn't wake up till ten o'clock the next morning. Sophia
was sitting by his side.

'Hello, darling, how long have you been awake?' he said when
he woke up.

Sophia looked the way she sounded—very tired. 'I dozed off a
couple of times, but I kept waking up!'

'Why don't you get a few hours in now?' Peter asked.

'Peter, listen to me, I have something to say to you. I want you to
understand what I'm saying and the importance of it, OK?'

Peter was taken aback by Sophia's words. 'Yes, all right, darling,
go ahead.'

Sophia put her arms out towards Peter. 'Give me a cuddle first.'

'You don't have to ask me for a cuddle,' he answered, taking her
into his arms. 'You can have a cuddle any time you like.' He held
her as he asked, 'Now what do you want to say to me?'

Sophia pulled herself away from him, looked straight into his eyes, and said, 'Peter, I have come to a decision. I am going to go back to Birmingham. I'm giving myself up to Brett.'

Before she could say any more, Peter had leapt off the bed and stood, staring at her in amazement. 'What are you talking about?' he shouted. 'Going back to that bastard, why? What's made you say that?'

'I'll tell you why, Peter. I have caused a lot of trouble for you, your close family, and your friends. I have not only caused them trouble, but also put them in great danger. I cannot allow it to continue, Peter. I love you too much for that!'

Peter listened with utter disbelief written on his face. He grabbed Sophia, wrapped his arms around her, and held her very tight. 'I have listened to you. Now I want you to listen to me. If you think for one second I would let you walk away from me, unless it was because you didn't want to stay with me any more, then you just don't know me, Sophia! First, you have not caused any trouble for anyone. Brett Carlodo is the one that's caused all the trouble. And secondly, if you went back to Birmingham, you know damn well what would happen . . . he would kill you. You know that, I know that. It's not a maybe either. It's a fact!'

Sophia started to cry, and through her tears, she said, 'Peter, my darling, I know all that you have said is true, but you have got to realise the danger you are in. How do you think I could carry on living if anything happened to you because of Brett's actions? Do you really think, after last night's fiasco, he is going to give up on me? Well, I know him, and it is going to make him all the more determined. He will now stop at nothing until he achieves what he's sat out to do! And that is to get his revenge on the both of us.'

'Yes, I agree with everything you have said,' replied Peter, 'but this is a war that we are going to win. I happen to think that what we have found together is worth more than anything else in the world. And I'll tell you this, Sophia, my darling, there is nothing or no one on this earth that would ever change my mind about that! So no matter what form your argument takes, the answer, as far as I am concerned, will be the same. You're not going anywhere!'

Sophia held on to Peter as she whispered, 'All right, Peter, I do feel the same as you do, and I agree we are in this together now. If we don't come out of this, I just hope we go as one.'

'It won't come to that, Sophia, we are going to beat these bastards, believe me, we will!'

CHAPTER 23

CHANGE OF TACTICS

Brett Carlodo was holding, what to him was a very important gathering of his most 'loyal' workers. He had asked them all to come along because he wanted to bring the whole saga of the 'slut nurse Sophia' to a conclusive end. Having already spoken to Harry and Phil, regarding the disastrous outcome at 'Dale Farm', he had decided on a more direct approach.

'Right, gentlemen, there is a very pressing problem that needs to be addressed. I do not need to tell you that I will stop at nothing when it comes to getting back something that has been taken and what I think is rightfully mine!' Brett looked at each member in turn. 'It has come to my attention that one or two of you are not happy with the way I run my business! So I would like the person or persons to stand up and be counted, if of course he's got the guts.'

The twenty or so men in the room started looking at each other, moving their feet about, nervously scratching heads, generally sending out all sorts of messages to the watchful eyes of the boss.

'I received a message late last night, from the people who organise, distribute, and run the networks in this country,' Brett continued. His face was starting to take on a different hue as he spoke. 'We are talking about the people that pay you your money every month! The people that keep you in luxury lifestyles! And the message was loud and clear. They said they don't like what they are hearing about me, they said that I am drawing too much attention to the people we do business with, and until I can prove that things are back to normal, it's "don't call us, we'll call you", which upsets me more than I can say! Because it is going to restrict my operations very severely, which means it's going to affect you too. Now what I thought was very nice of them was that they chose to name the person who had the bloody audacity and, in this case, the absolute stupidity to shit on his own doorstep.' At this stage, Brett got up out of his chair, walked round to the front, and started to thread his way between the seats.

'Now is anyone going to stand and own up, and maybe, just maybe, we can work something out, the alternative? Well, the culprit won't have to worry about that or anything else for that matter! Isn't that right, Sammy?'

Sammy was sitting in the second row from the back. He was forty-five years of age, a divorced petty criminal, and had worked for Brett for three years. He was not very bright but useful. He suddenly looked up and stared at Brett. 'Sorry, boss, what?'

'Sammy, during the time you have worked for me, have I ever treated you badly, kept you short of money?'

Sammy was holding contact with the floor as he answered, 'No, boss.'

'Then why did you go running to other people and say you thought I ran things like a mad man?'

'I'm sorry, boss, I must have been drunk at the time.' Brett was now standing directly behind Sammy.

'Yes, Sammy, so am I sorry.' Brett then reached over, clasped his left hand over Sammy's mouth, and held it with a vice-like grip. With his right hand, he pulled a knife and slowly pushed it into and through Sammy's neck. His spinal cord severed, his legs kicked out straight, and he died very quickly. Brett straightened up, left the knife where it was, and casually sauntered back to his desk and sat down, as though he had just been to the toilet.

'Now as I was saying, this matter has to be resolved, and this is how it is going to be done.

'Phil, Snouty, Harry, and Reggie, you are to go down to Paglesham in Essex and get hold of the little girl, Josie I think her name is. She is the daughter of that Peter Doddington. When you get her, take her to the factory in Stratford. Let me know when you're there and I'll come up. But I don't want anyone hurt, I want that privilege. Any questions?'

They all sat there in utter silence, as though struck dumb by the callous behaviour of the madman standing in front of them.

'Right then, meeting closed.'

Phil and Harry had arranged to meet up with Snouty and Reggie in Paglesham.

Phil was driving. They had just joined the M25. Phil took a chance on Harry.

'I am not very happy about this, Harry,' he said.

'Say what's on your mind, Phil,' Harry replied.

'I've seen some things in my time, Harry, but what he did today takes the biscuit. Just between ourselves, I think he's completely lost it!'

'Well, I'm pleased you have said that, Phil,' answered Harry, 'because I thought the same but I was frightened to say anything to anybody. The trouble is, Phil, you don't know who the hell to trust.'

'Yes, I agree,' said Phil, 'but how do you know if you can trust me, mate?'

Harry threw Phil a very nervous sideways glance.

'I hope you're joking with me, Phil!'

'You see, Harry, my son, you don't really know if what I have just said is a set-up, just to make you open up and tell me what you really think about Brett Carlodo. Ha! Ha! Ha! And what would you say, if I told you I had recorded our conversation?'

'I would say you are a right devious bastard, and that you are beginning to get on my bloody nerves. And just for the record, Phil, you don't know if I'm trustworthy either, so we are both in the same basket. If I go down, you come with me.'

'All right, Harry, you don't have to be so shirty, I was only joking.'

Harry was tight-lipped.

'Well, I wasn't, OK?'

No one spoke for the next thirty minutes. Then Harry asked, 'Do you know the penalty for kidnapping a child?'

Phil grimaced, visibly frightened.

'To be honest with you, Harry, it's not the penalty that I'm worried about. It's what Brett's got in store for us if we mess this one up!'

Harry nodded his head in agreement.

'Yes, and if we back off now, we could go the same way as Sammy! My motto has always been survival of the fittest.'

The traffic on the M25 was as thick as ever. It took three and a half hours to complete the journey from Birmingham to the village of Paglesham. It was 6 p.m. The day had been very warm for the time of the year; the temperature had reached the low twenties, which was very unusual for early May.

The four-man team met up in the local pub to work out the best way to go about the snatch. The information regarding Shirley's movements, which both Phil and Harry were able to put into the pot were of great help.

It was known what time Shirley left her house to take Josie to nursery school for instance. And the time she picked her up. Also, when the weather was nice, Phil, had noticed Josie playing in the front of the house in the garden. Sometimes Shirley was seen going to her mother's house in Stock, dropping little Josie at a friend's on the way. After some discussion, it was agreed between them that the best form of action, and indeed the safest way of conducting the operation, was to take her when she was on her own. They would need the extra time because of the geographical layout of the village. There was only one way out. If the alarm was raised too soon, the gang would stand no chance of getting past Southend-on-Sea, let alone getting to London!

The next day was fine and sunny. The four men were positioned near Shirley's house, both cars partially hidden by the trees. Shirley intended meeting David at about eleven o'clock, to go and see Rene, so she planned to drop Josie off at Jessie's around ten, as the nursery was not open.

'Mummy, mummy, look there's a Robin outside, on the fence. It's got a red jumper on. Shirley came to the window and placed her head up close to the little girls. And sure enough, there was a little Robin perched on the fence cocking his head to one side and seemed to be looking at Josie!

Shirley put her arm round her daughter and laughed. 'Well done, darling, clever girl, yes, you're right, that's a little Robin.'

Josie giggled with excitement as the Robin flew off. Josie jumped off the window seat and ran into the kitchen where her mother was filling the dishwasher.

'Mummy, can I go in the garden and play?'

Shirley closed the dishwasher and turned round to face her daughter.

'No, darling, we are going round to Auntie Jesse's in a minute, and then you can go in her garden.'

Josie laughed. 'All right, Mummy.' And she skipped away. Shirley placed her mobile back in her bag; she had just told David she was about to leave and that she'd be there in half an hour.

'Is that grandad, Mummy?' Josie asked inquisitively.

'Yes, darling, now come on, we're going now.'

Phil and company watched as Shirley and her daughter left the house, got in their car, and drove off.

The men made no attempt to follow, as they all knew where Shirley was heading.

Jessie Saunders lived in a modern house in Rochford. She was a typically modern women; she was completely in tune with all things modern, even her marriage would be seen by some to be ultra-modern. Her husband lived with her, slept together, and even had the occasional copulation. But mainly it was with other people they both had sex with. They were swingers, and they didn't care who knew it. They enjoyed their life. Five foot five inches tall, overweight, and not bad looking, she possessed an over-the-top personality, which some people could only take in very small doses. She and Shirley had been friends since their school days; she was a very good mother to her three children, and Shirley felt very relaxed about Josie staying with her.

An hour after Shirley left her house, two cars moved off together and headed in the direction of the village of Rochford, about three miles from the Thames Estuary town of Southend–on-Sea. The time was 11.15 a.m.

Two of Jessie's three children were at school. Her youngest, William, was out in the front garden, playing with Josie in an old car dumped on one side years ago. Jessie and one of her friends were in the lounge, laughing and sharing a joke over a glass of wine.

The occupants of a Land Rover were parked a safe distance away from the eyes of anyone in the house. Phil and Harry had already noted Josie playing without proper supervision, virtually delivering her into their hands.

William got out of the old vehicle and shouted to Josie, 'I want to go to the toilet, Jo.' He ran into the house. Harry quickly walked over to where she was happily amusing herself with the steering wheel. Harry got a bar of chocolate out of his pocket and approached the little girl.

'Hello, sweetheart,' he spoke softly, 'do you want some sweeties?'

'Yes, please,' replied Josie, getting out of the car and running over to where Harry was standing. Josie was quite at ease with the nice man who was giving her some chocolate. She took Harry's offered hand and trotted off with him. Phil was ready with the car door already open. Josie got in the back seat and settled down as the car drove off.

Harry was driving again. Phil was on the phone to Brett. It was picked up after thirty seconds. Brett sounded breathless.

'Yes, Phil, what you got for me?'

Phil was excited as he answered, 'Good news, boss, we've done the business. No problems, so far.'

'Well done, Phil, carry on as arranged, I will meet you there in about four hours. Any hiccups, call me, OK?'

'All right, boss, will do.'

Josie sat eating her chocolate looking out of the window.

'Where's Willy?'

'We are going to pick him up later,' Harry answered.

'Where's my Mummy then?' Josie asked.

Phil intervened, 'We are going to take you to your mummy now, all right, darling?'

Josie was satisfied with that answer and appeared to accept her lot.

The two vehicles were approaching the end of the forty-mile an hour speed limit on the A127 at the boundary line between the borough of Southend and Rayleigh, where the limit increased to fifty. About two hundred metres ahead, Harry suddenly started cursing. Phil looked up and did the same. What they saw nearly gave them both a heart attack! Two police cars were blocking the nearside lane, stopping cars at random. Phil spoke first.

'Don't panic, Harry, they are not stopping everyone!'

Harry was frozen; he didn't answer. They both held their breath as they drew level; the car in front was pulled in. Harry was forced to brake to avoid a collision; the car pulled over. The police officer looked at Harry and waved him on. Harry put his foot down on the gas.

"Steady on, Harry, don't attract attention! Now let's get there as quickly and as safely as possible.'

CHAPTER 24

THE CRY OF GRIEF

Rene was being discharged from hospital after a four-week period, feeling much better. David and Shirley were with her to bring her home, where David intended to move in permanently to make sure she was properly cared for. Shirley opened the front door of her mother's house. David came behind, giving Rene a helping hand.

'Don't fuss, David, I can walk you know!'

David smiled to himself. That sounded more like the old Rene, he thought. David sat with a hot cup of tea beside him. Shirley was in the kitchen with her mother. It suddenly occurred to him that Shirley was still ignorant of all the facts regarding Peter and Sophia. He knew that somehow she would have to be told the truth. He worried how she would take the news that they had lied to her all this time. Even her own mother had lied, to protect her feelings, which David knew she would not accept as an excuse. The sound of her laughter floated from the direction of the kitchen. He decided this was not the best time for it any way.

Jesse was on her third glass of wine, feeling happy. Her son William came in from the garden and stood by his mother.

'Hello, darling, do you and Josie want a drink?'

'Yes, please, Mummy,' he answered.

'Go and fetch Josie, darling,' said Jesse.

'No, Mummy, I can't,' he answered.

'Oh, go on, Willy, do it for Mummy!'

'I can't, Mummy, cos she's not there any more.'

Jesse was on her feet in a second, and her friend Wendy was right behind her. Jesse was shouting out Josie's name before she hit the garden. In utter panic, she took in the area of the front garden in one glance and instinctively knew that something terrible had happened to her friend's baby. Continuing to call her name, she ran out into the road. A car had to take evasive action to avoid a collision. She heard herself shouting at the driver, 'Have you seen a little girl in the road?'

The man could see that Jesse was very distressed.

'How long has she been gone?' he asked.

Jesse carried on down the road without giving the man an answer to his question, still calling out 'Josie! Josie!'

Wendy caught hold of Jesse's arm and suggested, 'Come on, Jesse, we had better go home, William is on his own.' It made Jesse start to think again. She reacted to her friend's words and turned back. 'Let's ask William if he saw where she went,' Wendy suggested as they both ran towards the house.

William was sitting outside on the grass when they got back.

Jesse took hold of both his hands and knelt down beside him.

'Willy, darling, where did Josie go? Tell Mummy.'

William looked at his mother and said, 'Mummy, why are you crying?'

Jesse ignored him.

'William, where is Jesse?'

'Indoors I think,' he giggled.

Wendy appeared from behind and said, 'No, Jesse, she's not in the house, I've just searched from top to bottom.'

'Then we have to call the police, Wendy!'

'I think we should hang for a while when we search around a bit more. She could be in a neighbour's house,' Wendy advised.

'Yes, you could be right, Wendy. But I had better let Shirley know what's happened.'

'Just try and calm down, Jess, we don't want to send Shirley into a blind panic, she's got enough on her plate at the moment.'

'It's all right for you to say keep calm, Wendy. It was me that was supposed to be looking after her.'

'OK,' said Wendy, 'get in touch with Shirley and let her know that Josie has gone missing. Do you know where she is?'

'Yes, she should be at her mother's by now. She was meeting her father–in–law at the hospital and bringing her mother home today.'

'Then ring her now, let her know what's happened.'

Jesse stood looking at the phone. She was shaking from head to toe; she felt as though she was going to pass out any second, wrestling with the thought of how she was going to tell her friend that her little girl was gone!

'Well, go on then, phone her,' urged Wendy.

'I am, I am, I'm just trying to think what to say,' cried Jesse, as she picked up the phone. She quickly dialled Shirley's mobile.

Shirley shouted from the confines of the downstairs cloakroom.

'David, that's my phone ringing, can you get it please.'

'Yes, OK.' David picked up the mobile from the kitchen table, put it to his ear, and said, 'Hello, this is David Doddington on behalf of Shirley.' There was a pause, and then he said, 'Oh hello, Jesse, how are you? Shirley won't be a minute . . . . What? What do you mean gone? How long?' There was another pause.

'Well, have you looked everywhere?' Another long pause.

'My God, the bastards! Nothing . . . I was just talking . . . no, it's too early to call the police. I'll tell Shirley, stay where you are in case she turns up! We'll come down. Yes, all right, bye.' David, for once in his life, could not easily make a decision. He knew if he let them call the police, it could put little Josie's life in danger because he was in no doubt at all that this was the work of Brett Carlodo.

Shirley came into the kitchen.

'Who was it, David?' she queried.

David's brain worked overtime. 'Err, oh, it was only Tony about the insurance on the car.'

'What about the car insurance?'

'Nothing, he's just told them to take his name off the policy,' David lied.

'About time too,' said Shirley. She followed David into the lounge where Rene was resting.

'I won't be long, my sweet,' he said to Rene, 'I'm just going to get some petrol while Shirley is here with you.'

'That's all right, David, I'll be OK!'

David drove the car out of sight of the house and pulled over to one side. He dialled Peter's number.

He was trying to control the anxiety in his voice as he spoke, 'Peter, I have some very bad news, I need to get you, Tony, and the boys together and meet up somewhere, very quickly, at the White Horse in half an hour.'

Peter sounded frightened, 'Dad, what's happened? Tell me!'

'I can't tell you over the phone, Peter, goodbye.'

David went back to the house and told Rene and Shirley he needed to go out for about an hour. He asked whether Shirley would wait till he got back before she went home.

'Yes, that's all right, David,' she agreed.

David went straight to the White Horse Pub in Billericay. Tony and the rest of them were already there. Tony jumped up from his chair as soon as David came through the door.

'David, what is this all about?'

David stood just inside the pub. 'Peter . . . Tony . . . they have taken little Josie.'

Peter was the first to respond, 'What? What are you talking about, Dad? Who's taken her?''My God! They haven't, no, not my little girl!' Tony had turned white. 'David, I swear, I'll kill the bastards!'

'Where's Shirley?' asked Peter.

'Shirley's at her mum's house, and she knows nothing about it at the moment,' replied David.

'Why have you not told her, David?' asked Peter.

'Because she will go straight to the police, and you know who we are dealing with. Somehow, we have got to wait until we hear from Brett Carlodo.' David continued, 'Failing that, we will all go back to Rene's house and lay it on the line, tell Shirley everything that's happened from the start, but before we do that, I think we should all take on-board the mighty injustice we have inflicted on her over the last three months. And I am one of the biggest culprits. I have blatantly lied to her several times, albeit to save her feelings. But now with hindsight, I am beginning to think I should have let the truth come out from the start.'

Peter turned to Sophia, who was putting her coat on. 'Sophia! What are you doing?'

'Peter, I have got to get out of here, this is all my fault. I am not going to put a little girl's life in front of mine for anyone, I'm sorry, darling, not even for you!'

Tony intervened, 'Sophia, she's my baby. I agree you can't put yourself before Josie. But listen, we have to wait to hear from that bastard of a human being before we do anything! He will definitely be getting in touch to give us his demands. Then, Sophia, only then, can we decide what to do.'

Peter joined in, 'He's right, Sophia, not only that, if you think I would let you go on your own to face him, you don't know me like you think you do. Whatever happens, we see this through together.'

Kevin spoke to everyone, 'Well, I may not be the brightest star in the sky, but I know one thing for sure. Shirley has got to be told her little girl has been snatched.'

'Yes, I agree, Kevin,' David said. 'But first of all, we have to tell her what led up to this in the first place. Once she knows everything, she will understand why it is important not to call the police.'

Peter was standing with his arms around Sophia.

'Then do we all agree that we go back with Dad to Rene's, come clean about everything, and just wait to hear from Brett?'

All said it was the best idea. Just as the last one came out of Margie's house, Sophia's mobile sounded off. Peter took it out of his side pocket, and it was Brett calling. Peter held up his hand to indicate to the others to be quiet.

'Hello.'

'Ah, could I hazard a guess and say I was talking to the elusive Mr Doddington after all this time?' Brett's voice was cold and slimy.

Peter could not help feeling a mixture of fear and anger as he replied, 'Yes, this is Peter Doddington. How can I help you?'

'You're a cool one, I'll give you that, but you can be as cool as you like, matey. I know the fix you are in. If I was in your position, I would try and do something about it. So I think you have been waiting for this call to enable you to form a plan. Am I right, Peter?'

'What do you want, Carlodo?'

'Oh, you can call me Brett, Peter. I'll tell you exactly what I want.'

Brett's voice took on a more sinister tone.

'You and that slut of a girl that I trusted will come down to an address in East London and present yourselves to me. The little girl will then be released.'

'And if I do not wish to do your bidding?' asked Peter.

Brett was becoming impatient.

'Look, I am not asking you, I am telling you, scumbag, to get down here as fast as you can. If you do not do as I tell you, I will cut off your daughter's head and send it to you wrapped up in a sheep's cloth!

'Anyone who knows me would tell you that I never make false promises. I always do exactly what I say I am going to do. Just to make sure you believe what I'm saying, I will cut off the little finger of her right hand and send it to you. How will that suit you?'

Peter nearly passed out when he heard those last words.

'Please, I beg of you, if you have one ounce of decency left in you, don't hurt my little girl. I'll do anything you want, I'll bring Sophia with me as soon as you tell me where!'

'You see how easy it is, Peter. When you start to cooperate with me, things run quite smoothly. I've always considered myself a reasonable sort of chap. Now just so that you understand, if you try to double-cross me in any way, you can be rest assured you will never see your daughter alive again. And, of course, that includes calling the police.

'To prove to you I am a reasonable man, I'll give you twenty-four hours to meet up with me. You will stand outside Stratford Rail Station at any time during the next twenty-four hours. There will be a man to collect you, is that clear?'

'Yes,' said Peter, 'perfectly clear.'

The phone went dead.

Peter held up his hands to stop the questions.

'Get to Rene's house. I'll let you know what he said when we get there.'

'All get in my Shogun, it's got seven seats,' said Tom.

CHAPTER 25

THE PRIDE OF JUDAS

When Phil and Harry arrived at the factory in Stratford, Brett was already there. Josie was asleep, so it was quite easy to cover her completely in a sheet and carry her across the factory floor without raising suspicion amongst the workers. Brett opened the security door leading to the room that gained entrance to the cellar. Harry held Josie in his arms, while Brett and Phil walked ahead down the corridor in the air-conditioned cellar. Brett unlocked the door at the end. Inside the small room, there was a bed, two chairs, and a table. On the table stood a double gas ring, connected to a bottle of propane gas, which stood in the corner. The opposite corner housed a toilet and washbasin. Brett turned to Harry.

'Put the kid on the bed, Harry. And, Phil, go to the shop and get whatever you need. You and Harry will be staying here for as long as it takes. I don't anticipate it will be very long. I'm leaving you the remote, Phil. You will need it to get out when I give you the call, is that all understood?' They both agreed. Brett turned and left the factory.

Phil and Harry sat on the chairs. They both felt very uncomfortable with the situation. Harry looked at the beautiful little girl lying there in front of him, her blonde curly hair falling over her eyes. Her little face was full of innocence, utterly oblivious to the terrible tragedy that had befallen her. Harry felt very guilty; he knew that what he had helped to do was one of the worst crimes in the book. Yet he dare not air his views to Phil; he felt he could not take the risk after the exchange of words on the way to Paglesham. It had shattered his trust in everyone. But he had come to one conclusion. He would never allow anything to happen to this little girl, even if it meant a showdown with Brett Carlodo! Phil broke his train of thought.

'What you thinking, Harry?' he asked.

Harry didn't look at Phil when he answered, 'I was just thinking about this little mite here, Phil.'

'Why? What about her?'

Harry carried on, 'Well, just look at her lying there, you must feel a little bit for her, for Christ's sake!'

'Harry, what do you want from me? Brett is my boss, and I know, if I don't do as I'm told, then it is me that takes the can. So get this through the tiny piece of matter that you call a brain, I don't give a shit who gets hurt as long as it's not me! Now that's spelling it out for you, Harry. To be quite honest, you're starting to make me a bit nervous. Perhaps I should ask the boss for someone else to take your place? Eh, what do you reckon, do you want me to do that, Harry?'

'I'll tell you what, Phil, I think you and Brett Carlodo came out of the same shell. You're both without any human emotions or empathy for anyone else but yourselves. And there's something else you should remember. As soon as you do anything that doesn't suit him, he will get rid of you as quick as he got rid of Sammy. You know that, as well as I do. It doesn't matter how much you suck up to him either.'

Phil was staring at Harry. He got up from his chair, walked over, and stood close to him.

'You, Harry, have been rubbing me up the wrong way for some time now, and I'm getting mighty pissed off with it. When I get pissed off, Harry, I do something about it! So shut the fuck up.' With that, he swung his open hand catching Harry across the left side of his face, knocking him off his chair. Harry rolled over the floor, slightly stunned by the force of the blow. Phil went back to his chair and sat down as though nothing unusual had happened.

Harry dragged himself to his feet and spoke in a soft voice, 'You are going to be very sorry you did that, Phil, that's a promise.'

'Yeah, I've heard it all before, mate, so shut it.'

A little moan coming from the bed diverted their attention. Josie was beginning to stir. She opened her eyes and looked around with a look of bewilderment.

'Mummy, Mummy!' she cried out. 'Where's my mummy gone?'

Harry knelt down beside her bed.

'All right, darling, Mummy will be here in a minute,' he said in the softest voice he could muster.

'Are you hungry, Josie?'

'Yes, I want to go to the toilet.'

'Of course, you can go to the toilet, dear.' Harry helped her off the bed.

'There we are, darling, it's over there.' Josie ran over to the toilet, went in, and shut the door.

'Who's a proper little mother then?' said Phil with a sneer.

'This little girl needs a woman to look after her, you bastard.'

Phil laughed. 'When she comes out, I'll be a mother to her. I'll give her a bath in that sink.'

Harry jumped out of his chair.

'You lay one of your filthy fingers on her, and, Phil, I will kill you.'

Josie came out of the toilet, ran over to the bed, and sat down.

'I'm hungry, I haven't had my dinner yet,' she said to Harry.

'All right, sweetheart, we'll get you some dinner, can you go and get her something to eat, Phil?'

'Why can't you go and get it if you're so worried about her not eating?' Phil replied.

'I'll tell you why, Phil, because I don't trust her with you, and as far as I can remember, the boss gave you the remote so you could get in and out, and if he finds that you asked me to go, he won't be very pleased.'

Phil was looking very sullen, but he gave in more easily than Harry had expected. 'Oh all right, I'll get her a Big Mac.'

'Yes, and I'll have one as well,' said Harry. After Phil had left, Harry sat there looking at little Josie, who sat waiting patiently for her McDonald's, looking at an old picture magazine. Harry was trying to form a plan in his mind, having come to the decision to try and get information to the police and let them know what Brett had planned for Sophia and Peter when they eventually arrived at Stratford Rail Station. What Phil had just done to him was the last straw. He had been thinking for some considerable time now, and he had got to create an opportunity to be able to escape the clutches of Brett Carlodo. But that was easier said than done. One wrong move on his part, and he would disappear like so many others he had known who had tried to buck the system.

A thought suddenly crossed his mind. What if he took Josie out now? Would he have enough time before Phil got back? Then he remembered Phil had the remote. Without that, he wasn't going anywhere. At the moment, Harry could not see any way out of the mess he and Josie were in, and he knew that there would be an opportunity presenting itself sooner or later. He just had to recognise it and take advantage of it when it happened. Josie was staring at him. 'Where's my mummy?' she asked.

Harry was at a loss what to say to her. 'Mummy's gone shopping,' he said. 'She'll be back later.'

She seemed to be satisfied with that as she lay down on the bed. It was a good half an hour before Phil returned with the food. Harry made some tea while Josie had orange juice. They had just finished their meal when Brett came through the door.

'Is everything all right here?' he asked.

Phil answered, 'Yes, boss, everything's fine.'

'Ok, I'll see you in the morning.' And then he was gone.

Harry sat on the bed next to where Josie was lying. Phil sat in the chair opposite. Harry didn't like the way he was staring at the little girl. Phil suddenly got from the chair, walked over, and sat on the bed, at the same time shoving Harry to one side.

'Go and sit in the chair, Harry, I'll look after her now.'

'Oh no, you won't,' shouted Harry, trying to push Phil off the bed, without much success. Phil then elbowed Harry hard in the ribs, and Harry heard a distinct crack as one of his ribs gave way. The pain was excruciating. Harry staggered across the room, fighting for his breath. Phil followed him and punched him on the side of his head, knocking him on to the floor.

'Now, perhaps that will teach you not to meddle in my affairs,' he snarled, as he turned to walk back to the bed. Harry was up on his feet again, fighting the agony he was experiencing. With all the strength he could muster, he charged at Phil's back. The momentum carried them hurtling across the room. They both hit the bed. Phil drew a long bladed knife from a leg sheath. The combined weight of the two men tipped the bed on its end, throwing Josie and her minders on the floor. As they hit the deck, Harry heard a stifling sound coming from Phil's lips; he wasn't moving. Harry pushed himself up from the floor. Josie was screaming in the corner of the room. Harry turned Phil over. He could now see the knife sticking from his chest. Looking at it, Harry thought it must have cut his heart in half. He moved over to Josie.

'Come on, darling, the nasty man has gone now.' Harry cuddled her, and she began to quieten down. Harry straightened the bed and forced Phil's body under it.

CHAPTER 26

THE TRUTH WILL BE OUT

Having all piled into the Shogun, it didn't take long to arrive outside Rene's house. David led the way. Shirley opened the door.

'Hello, David, is everything all . . . ' she cut off in mid-sentence when she saw how many people were standing there. Peter and Sophia were the next ones in. Shirley was puzzled.

'What's going on, David?' she asked as she closed the door behind the last one. David waved his hand in the direction of a chair.

'Please sit down, Shirley, we've got something to tell you.' Everyone found a seat. Everyone was looking very nervous, for different reasons.

Shirley had focused on Sophia, wondering who she could be, and on Peter with utter surprise, because she thought he was in Devon.

'Hello, Peter,' she said. 'Nice to see you, how are you now? I thought you were in Devon!'

'Yes, thanks, Shirley, getting better every day,' Peter replied.

David felt he had to take control of the situation and cut this conversation short. 'Right,' he dived in, 'we are in the middle of a very serious and potentially life-threatening period of our lives. For Shirley and Rene's benefit, I am going to have to start at the beginning so that we are all aware of what led us into the situation we find ourselves in today!'

'First of all, Shirley, let me introduce you to Sophia. Sophia, this is Shirley, Peter's ex. Shirley, this is Sophia Andrews, Peter's girlfriend. She was his nurse at the hospital in Birmingham.'

Shirley desperately tried to hide the look of disappointment on her face at David's words.

She put out her hand and said, 'Oh, nice to meet you.'

'And you,' replied an equally subdued Sophia.

David went on to explain about the relationship between Sophia and Brett Carlodo and what sort of man he was, how he was involved in all sorts of criminal activities, and more importantly, what he was capable of doing to people if they refused to do his bidding. As Rene sat there listening, David could see she was beginning to get very upset.

'Rene, darling, are you all right?' he asked.

'Yes, David, please carry on, I just wonder where this is all leading to.'

'Well, I'm afraid it's not good news. His men have already tried to snatch Peter and Sophia from where they were hiding, but we managed to stop them in their tracks with, I might add, a lot of help from Tony's friends.

'But now things have taken on a completely different perspective. And this is very hard for me to say, Shirley, but today they took little Josie and—'

David got no further, as both Rene and Shirley jumped up from their seats.

'No, no,' Shirley was screaming, 'not my Josie.'

Rene grabbed Shirley and held on to her tightly. Rene turned her head to look at David. 'David, have you called the police?'

David answered quickly, 'No, no, we can't do that, Rene.'

'You haven't called the police!' screamed Shirley. 'Why not for goodness sake?'

'Shirley, we were warned not to.' David felt inadequate as he spoke.

Tony raised his voice above all the noise. 'Please, everyone, let me just explain something to you.' Suddenly he could hear himself speak. 'This is what is going to happen. Peter and Sophia have been told to go to Stratford Rail Station and wait there for someone to pick them up. Once they have been collected, Josie will be released unharmed.'

'What's going to happen to Peter and Sophia when those people get them?' asked Rene.

'We don't know yet,' replied Tony. 'The most important thing is to get Josie back where she belongs.'

Rene got up and walked out of the room without anyone noticing.

She went straight into her bedroom and locked the door behind her.

Taking her mobile from her handbag, she quickly keyed in the number. It rang for fifteen seconds. A firm deep voice responded with 'Yes.'

'Hello, this is Rene Staples.'

'Rene, my darling, how nice to hear from you, how are you?'

'I'm not too bad now, Douglas. But I had a little stroke a few weeks ago. But I am getting there.'

'Sorry to hear that, Rene, I hope you continue to improve. Now what do I owe this pleasure, after all this time?'

'Douglas, I need your expert help!'

'That's what I do, Rene, especially for such an old friend. Where shall we meet?'

'At my house, if that's all right.'

'Yes, that's fine with me. When?'

'Yesterday, that's how urgent this is, Douglas!'

'I'll be there in two hours.'

'Douglas, thank you, I look forward to seeing you very much.'

CHAPTER 27

SERIOUS INTERVENTION

Douglas Norman Anderson was born of immigrants from Barbadas, who had settled in England in 1970 and given birth to him two years later.

He had an excellent childhood including fine comprehensive education, finishing at Cambridge University as a top-class structural engineer. He joined the Green Berets and passed out as one of their finest recruits. After seeing action in Northern Ireland and helping to get rid of Saddam Hussein, he trained for the SAS, and again, passed every part of the course with flying colours, ending his career as major. He then formed his own team of ex-SAS members, and now, after five years, was in great demand by governments all over the world. Needless to say, he came as very, very, expensive. At six feet two inches tall with a body honed like a fine piece of art, black hair cropped short, with looks that would put Sean Connery to shame, he remained single. Never had the time!

Rene shut the phone down and stood in the middle of the bedroom, her mind racing. Had she done the right thing? Calling on the services of one of the most professional people in the field of covert operations, not that Rene Staples was unfamiliar with the world of shadowy espionage and intrigue. She was still bound under the oath of the Official Secrets Act, but no one could take away the memories of those far-off days of excitement. She first set her eyes on Thomas Staples (No.cssx858828) when working as a liaison officer for M15, coordinating operations between themselves and other governments, mainly the CIA. In those days, Tommy was a very good-looking young man, who was recruited straight from university into training for M15. He spent the next thirty years serving his country in all parts of the world, constantly putting his life on the line. Rene knew the nature of all the operations he was sent on, knew that he may never come back from any one of them. But she still married him in a secret wedding within three years of their first encounter. It was on one of those covert operations that Tommy and Douglas came together and formed a trusting friendship that lasted up to the day Tommy passed away two years ago. Rene still remembered the last words Douglas had said to her before leaving after the funeral service. 'Rene, if you ever need my help, you call me straight away and I'll be there for you!' Rene dragged herself back to reality and prepared herself for the explanation she would need to come up with, to convince the others that she had done the right thing.

She walked into the room to find that her daughter was still in tears. The others trying to console her were not having a lot of success. All Shirley kept saying was, 'call the police'. Everyone looked up at Rene as she walked into the room. David came over and took her by the arm.

'Where have you been, darling? I was beginning to get a bit worried! Come and sit down.'

'No, David, I have something to say to everyone. Please all listen very carefully to what I am going to say.' Everyone there suddenly went quiet, waiting in anticipation, wondering what she was going to say.

Rene stood and clasped her hands together, looked at each one in turn, and said, 'What I am about to say will probably amaze everyone in this room, including my daughter. So here goes. In about two hours' time, something will happen that could have an effect on all our lives. I have asked someone, who I know very well to take over this situation. He is an ex-SAS officer who has proved to be so good at his profession that he is sought by countries all over the world to help sort out rebellions and internal conflicts.'

Peter was the first to react to Rene's revelations. 'Rene, how did you get mixed up with an SAS officer?'

'Because I used to belong to M15, and so did Tommy.'

David jumped to his feet. 'You mean you were a spy's?' he asked incredulously.

Rene paused before she answered, 'Yes, David, something like that, but I am afraid I cannot go into it any further, because of the Official Secrets Act.'

Shirley was gazing at her mother as though transfixed. 'Mum, you and Dad worked for M15?'

'Yes, darling, but it never affected you in any way. But because of the contacts I have made, I can get this sorted.'

'Will he get Josie back for me, Mum?'

'I can guarantee it, Shirley. Now, who would like a nice cup of tea?'

Shirley and Sophia got up together. 'No, you don't, Rene, you sit down, we'll make it,' Sophia said. 'Me and Shirley.'

Exactly two and a quarter hours after they spoke on the phone, there was a knock on the door. Peter opened it to find three men and a girl standing there. The men were all over six feet tall and well-built. He estimated they were all in their late thirties.

The black man spoke first.

'Good evening, sir, my name is Douglas Anderson, I have an appointment to see Mrs Rene Staples.'

'Good evening to you, yes, I think she is expecting you, come on in, you're very welcome.'

'Thank you,' he replied as he stepped over the threshold, followed by his entourage. Rene got up of the chair and walked slowly over to Douglas, and they met in the middle of the floor. They wrapped their arms around each other in true and genuine friendship. When they parted, there were tears in Rene's eyes. The memories of the past times with the three of them together were still very strong, as they should be.

CHAPTER 28

MANAGEMENT PAR EXCELLENCE

Douglas made sure everyone was seated and comfortable.
'Good evening, my name is Douglas Anderson,' he began. 'I have been requested by my dear friend Rene to help in what I think is a very nasty situation. My team and I are going to get it sorted and bring it to a satisfactory conclusion. And that's a promise. But we cannot achieve any kind of progress without the full cooperation of all concerned. So to start things moving, one of my assistants will be coming round to each person to take some personal details in order to keep a file on who they are and what their role is. When this is all over, the files will be destroyed. Is that understood? Good, now I would like to speak to Peter Doddington and Sophia Andrews please.'

Peter got up and walked over to Douglas with an outstretched hand. Douglas held his hand in a firm grip and said, 'Hello.' Sophia followed behind and greeted Douglas with a high five. They all sat down and kept their voices low, as instructed by Douglas.

'There will be a helicopter arriving shortly to take both of you to a safe location. Neither of you will know where you are, because you don't need to know. I now want you to leave the room and pack your things without speaking to anyone. Is that understood?' They both nodded their agreement, got up, and left the room. Douglas stood up and beckoned Shirley across. Although they had never met, he would have known who she was. She had her mother's good looks. Shirley sat opposite Douglas and wondered what he had got to say to her. She didn't have to wait long.

'Shirley, I know how worried and upset you must be about your little daughter, but let me put your mind at rest. Brett Carlodo, although a very dangerous and ruthless individual, has a very high regard for children. I have run into this man many times before. The Met Police have been trying to nail him for years. But because of the way he has built his empire, mostly by ruthless domination, people are too scared to come forward and give evidence against him. Not only that, he has also managed to take film of a lot of men with power in the city—men who have been stupid enough to risk all, by succumbing to their basic animal instincts, and getting caught, literally, with their trousers round their ankles. But I can give you the absolute guarantee that he will not harm Josie, no matter what he has threatened you with.'

Shirley was overwhelmed to hear those words from a man who knew what he was talking about.

'Thank you so much, Douglas, I feel a lot better now. When will I get my little girl back?'

'As soon as I locate her whereabouts, you will have her back home within the hour. Now run along, I have got work to do.' As promised, the chopper arrived and landed without mishap, in the field situated directly behind the house. With Peter and Sophia safely on-board, it took off for an unknown destination. Rene stood by the window, watching it disappear under the shadow of the wispy cloud-covered light of the half-moon.

David came up behind her, curled his arms around her waist, and whispered, 'Rene, you have blown me away tonight, you are an amazing woman. I thought I knew you, but now I feel I have just met another woman, a very exciting and fascinating women. And, Douglas, well, I have seen all sorts of management teams in my working career, but tonight, I witnessed a master class in management.'

Rene turned to face her fiancé. 'David darling, that's what he does. He gets things done, completely regardless of what, or who, gets in the way.'

The commanding voice of Douglas Anderson interrupted everyone's conversation, 'Please gather round, I need you all to listen carefully, because I will not be repeating it.

'As you have witnessed, Peter and Sophia have been taken to a safe place, and you can be rest assured, they are now safer than they have ever been in their lives. But the rest of you, I am sorry to say, are not. The reason that makes me make a statement so blunt and to the point is because I know the kind of man we are dealing with very well. And I need to impress upon you all the importance of being absolutely aware of that every minute of the day and night. Brett Carlodo is a schizophrenic, hardened, unemotional criminal. He is completely devoid of human empathy towards other people with one exception, that exception, under the current circumstances, turns out to be our one saviour. He genuinely loves children and would never allow them to be put into any danger while he is around. So to put your minds completely at rest over little Josie's kidnap, as I have already told Shirley, Josie is, at the moment, safer than any of you.'

Everyone in the room visibly took a deep breath, with a look of relief written on their faces. Douglas carried on in the same vein.

'I want you all to be vigilant at all times, I want you to be observant at all times, I do not want you to go out on your own, and I mean anyone, and just to emphasise the point, it includes the men! Now is that completely understood?' Douglas looked in turn at each person in the room to receive their assent.

'Good,' he said, 'I am leaving now. Rene is my contact, and she is the only person among this group who will have full knowledge of future progress. Everyone else is on a need-to-know basis. Is that accepted?' Again the same procedure of positive reaction was repeated. 'Oh, and just one more thing, I am not going to apologise for not introducing the rest of my team . . . they do not exist! Good bye, all.'

They walked briskly to the car and sped off into the night, leaving everyone in a daze of admiration.

CHAPTER 29

SUSPICIOUS ESTIMATES

Harry sat looking at little Josie, who was sound asleep, curled up into a little ball on the old bed. Phil's feet could be plainly seen sticking out. Harry was trying to sort out, in his mind, just what he was going to tell Brett. He didn't have to wait very long. At exactly 0900hrs, the floor above the cellar slid silently across its grooves, and Brett Carlodo came waddling through the door, with Snouty and Reggie in tow.

Brett stood halfway in the room.

'What's been going on here, Harry?' Brett asked, moving Phil's foot with a kick.

'He tried to interfere with the girl, boss. I had to stop him, and he fell on the knife!' Brett stared at Harry for a moment, glanced down at Phil's body, and kicked it with all the force of his thick thighs—twice.

And each time, he said, 'Bastard, bastard!'

'Well done, Harry, you've saved me the job.'

'Right, Harry. Snouty, and Reggie are going to take the girl to the warehouse, the one near Colchester. You can go back to Birmingham and wait till I call you, you got that, Harry?'

Harry got up and said, 'Yes, boss, I got it.' He quickly left the factory. The men took Josie to the local McDonald's, where they all had breakfast and then proceeded to head towards Colchester in a black Mercedes limousine. Brett gave instructions to the driver over the intercom and settled back in the luxury of the black leather seat.

None of the occupants noticed the House Maintenance Contractors' van that inconspicuously fell in line about four vehicles behind. All who studied the van's exterior would have arrived at the same conclusion that it was what it looked like—an old maintenance vehicle, looking a bit tatty round the edges. The interior was a different thing altogether. Fitted out by professionals, there was an array of high-tech equipment laid out in sections and panels, computer screens, and surveillance satellites. Three men and a woman sat in front of the screens communicating with another source. One of the men was talking into a microphone.

'Yes, chip is in place, and we are dropping back by one mile.'

Douglas Anderson replied, 'Roger, keep us informed. Over and out.'

Brett Carlodo used his mobile to call Simon Rafferty.

'Hello, Simon, glad I got you, I want you to get information on all of Peter Doddington's relatives, for instance his father, his friends that live on Dale Farm in Billericay. And I need them as soon as possible, got it, Simon?'

Simon had no choice but to carry out Brett's instructions, to the letter.

'All right, I'll get on it,' he replied reluctantly. Brett cut him off and dialled a new number. It picked up; a girl answered from his Birmingham office.

'Gold Star Enterprises, can I help you?'

'Yes, please, put me through to Helen Jones.'

'Certainly, sir, can I ask who's calling?'

'Brett Carlodo.'

'Oh, sorry, Mr Carlodo, I'll put you through.' The extension rang twice.

'Hello, Brett.'

'Helen, I want you to trace the whereabouts of a mobile phone.'

'Yes, of course, what's the number?' Brett relayed Sophia's number.

'Let me know when you get a result. Goodbye.'

Nestling down at just above sea level, just across the River Thames from Canvey Island, there lies the old town of Leigh-on-Sea. It had been, in its hay day, one of the busiest ports in the country where the tall ships unloaded their precious cargos of silks and spices. Now it was just a tourist curiosity. It was also the temporary home of Peter Doddington and Sophia Reynolds. Anchored about a mile off the shore in an old Thames Barge, they were completely isolated from all and sundry, until Sophia answered her mobile phone without thinking and promptly gave their position away.

The limousine cruised down to the warehouse without interruption.

Josie was given dinner, and Brett kissed her on the cheek as he tucked her up in bed and said, 'Good night, darling.' Snouty and Reggie waited for the call. It came at about 11 p.m.

Brett immediately called upon people he could trust (they were on his payroll). They were instructed to go down to the old town at Leigh and bring Peter and Sophia back to the warehouse.

At around midnight, two cars came down Leigh Hill and headed for the Old Town High Street. They came quietly over the bridge into the cobbled road, past the Crooked Billet, and into the car park of the Peter Boat Inn. The headlights were switched off. The occupants sat peering into the half-light. The moon spread a yellow cloak over the flat calm sea that lay before them, showing the silhouette of the old

Thames Barge tugging at the anchor chain in a strip of deep water called the Ray. There were four men in each car. They sat there for another hour, got out, and lifted a package from each boot. A quick pull on a plastic ring attached to a cord produced two inflatable boats, complete with outboard motors. Launching the boats from a nearby ramp, they quickly jumped on-board. The muffled sound of the engines crackled into life as they sped off in the direction of the barge. Each of the men was armed with an automatic pistol and dressed entirely in black, ready to handle any unwanted opposition. Each man knew their brief: to seek out and retain both parties, no harm or physical injury, taking them back to the warehouse near Colchester. It took exactly three minutes to reach their destination. Each boat pulled alongside, and two men from each boat leapt aboard. Peter was the first to hear that someone had invaded the boat. Jumping out of bed, he quickly grabbed hold of the baseball bat that lay down beside the bed and raced towards the door. He didn't even make it to the handle; a crashing sound from the skylight above his head drew his eyes upwards. He just had time to catch a figure flying through the air before hitting him in the back and knocking him to the deck gasping for breath. Before he could recover, his hands were forced behind his back and handcuffs were snapped on his wrists. Meanwhile, Sophia had been likewise overcome. A strip of white tape was stretched over their mouth. It had been accomplished in just under one minute. Black covers were placed over their heads, reaching down to their waists. As the inflatables sped away from the barge, an LED suddenly came alive where the action had just taken place. It glowed for one minute and then went back as part of the starboard porthole. The two cars were on their way to join the A12, and the time was 1.15 a.m. A man in the lead car was talking to Brett Carlodo.

'Yes, mission completed, boss, no problems.'

'What do you mean no problems?' he repeated.

'Just what I said, boss, it was easy, they didn't have a chance.'

'All right, get back here as soon as you can.' Brett leant back in his chair, letting the words he had just heard turn over in his mind. (It was easy, they didn't stand a chance.) Something was wrong. Brett Carlodo had always listened very carefully to what his inner voice was saying to him. He was a great believer in basic animal instincts. The trouble was, he knew, it was only a feeling. So he told himself to be aware.

CHAPTER 30

Calculated Risk

The house phone had not completed its first ring before Rene had lifted it off its cradle and put it to her ear. She glanced at the wall clock and mentally noted it was 0430 hrs, as she said, 'Hello?'

'Hello, Rene, sorry to wake you, but something you should know,' Douglas Anderson sounded businesslike.

'That's OK, Douglas, what is it?'

'They have taken Peter and Sophia and are being monitored constantly. They are in no immediate danger. It's all under control.' That statement, coming from anyone else, would have put Rene in a state of utter panic. But coming from Douglas Anderson, she just acknowledged she understood, and her past training ensured she did not ask any questions. She just said thanks! But nevertheless decided it was time to get up, shower, and dress. David was still blissfully in the land of nod. Slipping on her dressing gown, she quietly disappeared into the en suite and closed the door.

Brett Carlodo studied the sheath of papers that had been sent to him from Simon Rafferty. Each sheet of paper contained details of Peter's father, David, his wife Shirley, his mother-in-law Rene

Staples, Tony Harman, and his brothers Tommy and Kevin. They had all caused him a great deal of aggravation, not to mention the loss of business deals he hadn't had time to deal with. In his perverted mind, he had a right to compensation. But he didn't want money, he wanted to put them away for good. That was the only way he could satisfy his revengeful lust for power. When they were dead, he would be the winner, the one on top, the one that held on to complete control. Subsequently, he ordered his men to round them up and bring them down to the warehouse.

Tommy and Kevin were out in their battered old lorry collecting unwanted kitchen appliances for scrap. They had had a pretty good day and were loaded fully with fridges, old cookers, and broken-down washing machines and were on their way to the scrapyard to turn it into money. Kevin was behind the wheel when suddenly a car pulled across the front of them. Kevin cursed and slammed on the brakes. The sudden stop shot a fridge and washing machine over the top of the cab and landed on top of the car! The impact crushed the driver's side, causing head injury to one of Brett's men. Kevin and Tom jumped out of the cab and ran to help the injured man. A crowd of people gathered round, most out of curiosity. Somebody called an ambulance and the police. They both arrived within five minutes of each other. Two police cars were in attendance, questioning witnesses, which appeared to be in abundance. The injured man was rushed off to Basildon Hospital, with the sirens and blue light flashing. The police had requested information on both vehicles from the DVLA and were waiting for a reply. One of the constables was questioning the passenger of the car who was sitting on the grass verge.

'Are you all right, sir?'

'Yes, Officer, I'm OK,' he replied.

'Can you tell me what happened, sir?'

'Well, no, I wasn't driving.'

'All right, sir, I will need to ask you some more questions later on.'

The officer then went over to the damaged car and looked inside. He opened the glove compartment and was surprised to see an automatic pistol lying there. He immediately called in on his mobile and requested back-up. Essex police responded with four armed units within ten minutes. They completely blocked the road in both directions causing havoc and gridlock to all the surrounding areas. Two armed police were sent to the hospital to guard the injured man. The passenger was searched and was found to be armed. He was promptly arrested and taken into custody for questioning. Kevin and Tom were also taken to Chelmsford Police Station. They were put into separate interview rooms. Tom sat opposite Detective Sergeant Beadle.

Beadle studied Tom for a minute, then said, 'Who were those men, Tom?'

Tom looked blank.

'What men?'

'You know the men I'm talking about, Tom, don't act simple, we know each other too well for that, don't we?'

'Yeah, I reckon we do, boss, at that,' said Tom.

'OK, so what's going on? It could be important!'

'Well, I must admit I am worried about all this, boss.'

Beadle leant forward closer to Tom.

'What are you worried about, Tom, tell me, and I might be able to help you!'

'It's about a bloke named Brett Carlodo. He's taken my little niece hostage—'

Beadle interrupted, 'Hold on, did you say Brett Carlodo?'

'Yes, that's right,' said Tom. Beadle immediately closed the interview and left the room. Knocking on the door of DCI Paul Jones, he went straight in and gave his chief the information.

'OK, get the names of each one involved from him. And then put together a comprehensive report and make sure it gets to me personally,' ordered the DCI. As soon as the door closed behind

Beadle, Jones made contact with New Scotland Yard, who immediately transferred him to special operations, who were currently building a case against Brett Carlodo, in collaboration with M15 which, if successful, would put him away for the rest of his natural life. The man in overall charge of the investigation was Commander Thomas Copeland, coming up for retirement within the next six months. He had been involved with Brett Carlodo's criminal career for the last thirty years. He had learnt during that time that to underestimate him could be very costly and dangerous. Brett Carlodo had slipped through Copeland's net many times in the past. But now, with the help of today's high technology and the experience gained from the past, the net was becoming foolproof. Commander Copeland knew that, very soon, his old enemy would be getting what he deserved. He said as much when he briefed his long time friend and colleague Douglas Anderson on the latest developments.

'Well, well, well, that's something I hadn't planned to happen,' said Douglas, when Copeland told him about the accident with the fridge.

'It just goes to show that not even the great Douglas Anderson gets it right every time!' the commander quipped.

'Maybe not, Thomas, but I guarantee the result will be the same,' countered Douglas.

'Can you bring me up to date? I need to get my men in position in good time,' said Copeland.

'They are already on site undercover, ready to make their move.'

'Yes, well everything's more or less gone to plan. Peter Doddington and Sophia Andrews, you know, have been taken. They should be there by now. My people are in close contact and ready for any emergencies.'

'Good, well done, Douglas. We acted on the information you passed on to us and subsequently carried out a dawn raid on the clothing factory, in the east end of London. It was like winning the lotto. Apart from the hard drugs with a street value of around 200 million, we found hard evidence of a major human trafficking ring, involving dozens of people from a variety of countries. It's going to take a few months to get all the evidence together, then of course, we will have the task of getting them all in the net!' Thomas laughed. 'I just hope I can do it before I retire.'

'Ok, Tom,' said Douglas, 'I'll see you down at the warehouse.'

David answered the door to Tony.

'Hello, Tony, what brings you here?' he queried.

Tony walked into the lounge, where Rene was sitting sipping a glass of wine. She got up from her chair and said, 'Hello, Tony!'

David and Rene stood, wondering what Tony was doing there.

They tried to snatch my brothers, David, but there was an accident and the police were involved. Tom told the police about Josie being taken by Brett Carlodo, so now the police are going to a warehouse where they have taken Josie, so now my daughter is in extreme danger.' Rene stepped forward.

'Don't worry, Tony, she is not in any danger.'

'What did you say?' asked Shirley as she came in from the kitchen.

'It's all right, darling, I know all about it,' said her mother.

Shirley raised her voice, 'No, Mum, it's not all right, if you know where she is, then I want to go there now!'

'Yes, and so do I,' said Tony. 'She's my daughter too, you know.'

Rene faced Tony.

'Look, Tony, Douglas has got this all under control. Any alteration to his plans could place everyone in danger, and mess the whole operation up.'

Tony was now angry. 'Well, I'm sorry to mess up your plans, Rene, but I am going, and you're going to take me!'

Shirley joined in with him and said, 'Yes, Mum, and me as well, if you don't take us, I'll never speak to you again!'

'All right,' said David.

'I think they are right, Rene, I think we should take them down there.'

Rene gave in with a sigh.

'All right, David, if you think so, but I'm going against my better judgement.'

The owner of the farm where the warehouse was situated had already noted some unusual activity around the fields adjacent to the warehouse, and it was making him a bit nervous. Although he knew a bit of Brett's history, he certainly didn't know what he was really capable of! He had a better idea after four armed police dressed in full combat gear confronted him in his living room and promptly handcuffed him, and one of them marched him away without making a sound. The other three proceeded to position themselves, strategically, giving them an uninterrupted view of the warehouse.

Brett Carlodo sat looking at Peter and Sophia, who were both tied to chairs that stood about ten feet from him with a sneer on his face.

'You bastards have caused me one hell of a lot of fucking trouble, and you are going to pay dearly for it. No one on this earth has had the nerve to treat me like you have done.'

Brett got out of his chair and walked over to them. He stopped when he was level with Sophia, raised his right hand, and swung it down hard across her face.

'That's how you are going to suffer for quite a while, until you ask me to kill you.' Sophia's chair was knocked across the floor by the force of the blow, and her head lay back resting on the back of the chair, with blood dripping from her mouth. Peter struggled to get out of the chair, and in the process, tipped over on to his back. Brett walked over and kicked him in the stomach. Peter's knees came up to his chin as he writhed in agony.

'You, bastard, untie me and I'll kill you!'

Brett responded by swinging his left foot in an arch and connecting with Peter's head, just below where the plate had been fitted. Turning to one of the four thugs in attendance, watching Brett at work, he shouted, 'Pick them up.' They rushed over and stood both chairs upright. Peter appeared to be unconscious, while Sophia was giving out little moans.

Brett spoke to the men, 'Keep guard over them. The two of you can get something to eat, then change places. They are not to be left alone.'

CHAPTER 31

CHANGE OF HEART

When Brett told Harry to go back to Birmingham, he got in the Land Rover, thankful he was out of the firing line, for the time being at least. After travelling for about an hour, he pulled in to a roadside cafe for something to eat. Sitting at a table by the window, he watched as people arrived and left in a more or less continuous flow. As he watched the men, women, and children come and go, he started to reflect on how he had missed out on his life. He had never been married or fathered a child, but spent the best part of his life behind bars. For what? Yes, he had managed to accumulate a bit of money, a few investments, bought his own house. But now he was starting to question himself, so, what had he really achieved in life? How many people had he actually helped along the way? The thoughts coming up in his head were seriously disturbing him. He couldn't think of one single moment in his life when he put someone else before himself. He had been indirectly involved in killings, extreme violence, and all sorts of other criminal activities as long as he could remember. And at fifty-four years of age, that was scary. Harry sat there for another half an hour, struggling to come to terms with his thoughts. At last he got up and moved quickly back to his car. Harry had made up his mind; he, at last, knew what he had to do. Joining the main carriageway of the M25, he headed back towards Colchester and the warehouse.

David was behind the wheel, with Shirley, Rene, and Tony keeping him company. They were fifteen minutes away from their destination.

Harry, in his Land Rover, was four cars behind as they approached the perimeter of the farm, when suddenly a police barrier stopped David's car in its tracks. Harry saw what was about to happen and quickly turned off the road. He knew the back doubles to the farm; he had spent a lot of time there in the past.

David got out of the car to talk to the policeman, and a voice behind him said, 'Hello, David, you know you shouldn't be here.'

Douglas Anderson looked over David's shoulder and saw Rene sitting in the car; he immediately walked over, bent down, and said in a low tone, 'Rene, it could only have been you that bought them here, and I am quite surprised about that.'

'Yes, Douglas, you are absolutely right. I know you have every right to be annoyed with me. I am bang out of order. But you must understand the pressure I am under. I am very worried about my granddaughter and my daughter.'

'All right, David, get back in the car and follow me,' said Douglas, as he instructed the barrier to be lifted. David followed him to where there was a small field a few hundred yards away from the farmhouse. Four police cars and two police buses were parked. There was no sign of their occupants. Douglas came over and said, 'Please, all of you stay in the car.'

Harry drove round the back of the warehouse and pulled up by the back entrance. Two of Brett's men were on guard; they both greeted Harry and stepped aside to let him pass. Harry walked through the passages until he was standing outside the room he knew would be holding Josie. He could hear voices on the other side of the door. He decided to take a chance. He opened the door wide and walked straight in, and was surprised to see Peter Doddington and Sophia Andrews tied up to chairs, but no sign of Josie! There were two guards sitting a few yards away. One of them got up as Harry entered.

'Hello, Harry,' he greeted him, 'we thought you were in Birmingham.'

'I was on my way, but I thought I might be needed here,' replied Harry. 'And now I am here, perhaps you can tell me what's going on with these two?'

'Sure thing, Harry,' the man replied.

'Brett told us to stay here with them till he got back.'

'OK, you can shove off now I'm here,' ordered Harry, 'and give yourselves a break for half an hour.'

'Thanks, Harry,' said the other man as he got up out of the chair, 'we'll leave them with you then!' They quickly scuttled out the door and left Harry on his own with Sophia and Peter. Harry rushed over to them and proceeded to untie them; he could see they both had been beaten.

Harry removed the tape from their mouths and said, 'Now listen to me carefully, I am going to get you out of here. Can you stand?'

Sophia answered, 'Yes, I think so, but I don't know about Peter.'

Peter groaned and said, 'I'm OK, just a bit of a headache, but I can walk.'

They moved out into the passage and were walking towards the back door, when suddenly one of the guards called out, 'Harry, where do you think you're going with them?' Harry turned round and saw the man running towards them with a gun in his hand. Harry dipped his hand into his coat, pulled out an automatic, and fired two shots very quickly. The man fell without a sound.

Harry shouted to Peter, 'Keep running, keep running.' They all ran as fast as they could until the three of them came out into the yard at the back of the building.

They saw the parked vehicles ahead of them and started to move towards them. They had just cleared away from the warehouse, when

Brett Carlodo suddenly appeared from the door of an outbuilding a little way ahead, with Josie in his arms and two of his men at his side.

'That's far enough, Harry! You, bastard, I thought I told you to go back to Birmingham.' As he screamed out at the top of his voice, Brett's face had tuned a shade of purple, and he had a gun in his hand. It was pointed at little Josie's head. His two men were also armed, and both had their guns trained on Harry, Sophia, and Peter.

'Put the gun down, Harry, unless you want her little head blown off!'

Everyone who heard the threat knew he meant what he said, with the exception of Douglas Anderson, who new Brett was bluffing. Immediately after Brett's warning, there came a heart-rendering scream.

'No, no, not my baby.' Shirley had managed to get out of the car when she saw Brett holding her daughter and was running towards him, screaming. Rene, David, and Tony were close on her heels.

Rene shouted to Shirley, 'Shirley! Think what you're doing, stop there.'

Shirley heard her mother's voice and came to a halt three yards from where Brett was standing.

She looked at Brett, tears clouding her eyes as she pleaded, 'Please . . . don't hurt my little girl.'

'Then tell him to throw the gun on the ground,' shouted Brett.

'You are the one who will put the gun down, Mr Carlodo, along with the rest of your people,' the voice of Commander Copeland rang out loud and clear.

'You are now completely surrounded. You have no chance of escape. No one will get hurt, if you lay your gun down now. You must see that your time has come at long last. You are wanted on at least three counts of murder, but I am arresting you on the kidnapping of one, Josie Doddington. You don't have to say anything, but anything you do say may be taken down and used as evidence.'

Brett responded with a tirade of obscenities aimed mainly at Sophia.

And then, with sweat now running into his eyes and his face contorted into overwhelming fury, he bellowed, 'You can all get stuffed, and you two bastards . . . ' He said pointing at Peter and Sophia, 'you have done me over, so here's your reward.'

With those words, he removed his gun from Josie's head and aimed it at Peter. Shirley saw what was about to happen, and without even having time to think about it, she threw herself between them. A very loud report of a gun echoed across the Essex Countryside. Four people fell to the ground. Brett's bullet entered Shirley's chest and passed through her body severing her spinal cord en route, then on exit, it hit Peter on his left shoulder, where it lodged near his collarbone. At exactly the same time as Brett pulled the trigger of his gun, a police sniper fired off a round which caught Brett Carlodo behind his left ear killing him instantly, twisting him round and landing him on his back. Josie, clinging on to his chest, was unhurt. The two men who had stood beside him immediately raised their hands high in the air in surrender as did Harry. Tony rushed forward and took Josie in his arms, trying to keep her eyes away from her stricken mother, while Peter struggled to sit up and cradle Shirley in the crook of his good arm. Shirley gazed into Peter's eyes and said, 'Sorry, Peter, I always loved you.' And then she died.

Rene stood looking down at her daughter's body, hanging on to David's arm, silently crying seeds of blame, already starting to grow inside her. Sophia bent down and helped Peter up on his feet, trying to stem the flow of blood coming from the wound. Douglas Anderson had already made sure there was an ambulance on site as part of his plan. Sophia, in her nurse's role, got into the ambulance with Peter and made sure he was comfortable as they roared off to the hospital.

The police arrested the rest of Brett's entourage and cordoned the whole area off. The main office in Birmingham, under the name of Gold Star Enterprises, which handled the money laundering, was raided, as was the factory in the east end of London, along with the human trafficking ring. It was one of the biggest successes in recent years for the Met.

Douglas Anderson stood with David who was consoling Rene. She was sobbing uncontrollably as she kept repeating, 'If I had done what Douglas had told me to do, she would still be alive.'

Douglas intervened, 'Rene, you cannot take the blame. Shirley did what she had to do.'

'And she saved Peter's life,' said David. Rene, starting to get herself together, looked up at David through her tears and asked, 'Who's going to tell Jamie? It will break his heart.'

'I think Peter will have to do that, Rene, when he comes out of hospital. He should be out tomorrow.'

A police sergeant approached them.

'Excuse me, I know this is a very sensitive time for you all, but I'm afraid I am going to have to take statements from each one of you.'

'Surely it can wait for a few days,' responded David.

'No, David, it can't,' said Rene. 'These things have to be attended to as soon as possible!'

'Thank you, madam. You're very understanding,' said the sergeant.

Peter lay in bed after coming out of surgery to have the bullet removed from his shoulder. Sophia was sitting beside him.

'This feels like déjà vu,' she said. 'It's where I came in, and do you know something, Peter? None of this would have happened if I had not got involved with you.'

'I knew you were going to say something like that, Sophia. I'm sorry to say you are talking a lot of rubbish.'

Sophia looked indignant. 'How can you possibly call it rubbish? It's true, isn't it?'

'Yes, it's true, and so is the fact that if Adolf Hitler had followed our army from Dunkirk, we would not be sitting here talking at all!'

'What's he got to do with us?' Sophia frowned.

'What I mean, darling, is that everything that happens to you alters the course of your life, people you meet, places you travel too, and there's nothing you can do about it, unless you are in possession of a crystal ball! If you were born with the gift of hindsight, you may be able to plan your life. But I very much doubt it.'

'Yes, I suppose you are right when you say it like that,' answered Sophia.

'Sophia,' said Peter, 'I know how terrible this has all been, not only for us, but for everyone that has been involved, especially Jamie and Josie. They have lost their mother. And Rene has lost a daughter. But thanks to a lot of loyal friends and relatives, we have got each other. And I think they all now need our help. Everyone of them has been traumatised to some degree because of us. So I think we owe it to them to help rebuild their lives in any way we can. Do you agree?'

'Of course, I do, Peter, we are now a full partnership. From now on we work together.'

'I'll talk to Tony about Josie and ask him if he wants her to live with us and Jamie,' said Peter.

'Yes, that will be a good idea, then he will be able to see her as much as he likes,' replied Sophia.

'How are you feeling now, Peter?' she asked.

'I feel a bit tired now,' he said, closing his eyes. 'But we haven't finished with Brett Carlodo yet, my darling.'

Sophia looked at Peter in amazement. 'Peter, he's dead now, how can he possible interfere with our lives any more?'

Peter was nearly asleep when he answered, 'Because he was shot dead whilst under arrest, and there's got to be an enquiry about that.'

'Don't worry about that now. Go to sleep, my darling, I'll be here when you wake up.' She bent and kissed him on the forehead.

EPILOGUE

The Devil's Inn looked daunting from the outside. Shirley was drawn to the large solid oak door. She didn't have to pause. Before she opened it, as she reached for the handle, the door swung wide. As she passed through the door closed behind her. She had taken about six steps, when she thought she heard the door creak open. She half turned and saw Brett Carlodo walk in behind her. A tall man with a black beard hurried over and said, 'I am the barman.'

'Go and sit over there,' he said, pointing to tables and chairs. 'I'll bring you a drink. You'll find your names on the chairs.'

'I don't want a drink, I want to go home to my children,' said Shirley.

The man looked at her and said, 'I'm sorry, my dear, no one ever leaves here, there is no way back. Well, having said that, there was one person that got away once, but I can't remember his name.'

Shirley found her allotted table and sat down staring into space. Brett Carlodo was sitting two tables away doing the same. The barman placed a glass of red wine on her table and walked away. He suddenly stopped, turned, and said, 'Oh yes . . . I remember his name now. It was Doddington, yes that was it, Peter Doddington.'

The End

CPSIA information can be obtained at www.ICGtesting.com
Printed in the USA
BVOW030955101111

275795BV00001B/31/P